Gilly & *the* Snowcats

GILLY & the SNOWCATS

R. S. Bovard

Mill City Press, Maitland

Copyright © 2016 by R.S. Bovard

Mill City Press, Inc.
2301 Lucien Way #415
Maitland, FL 32751
407.339.4217
www.millcitypublishing.com

All rights reserved. No part of this publication may be reproduced, stored in a retrieval system, or transmitted, in any form or by any means, electronic, mechanical, photocopying, recording, or otherwise, without the written prior permission of the author.

ISBN-13: 978-1-63413-758-4
LCCN: 2016914537

Cover and Interior Illustrations by Elisabeth Alba
Cover Design by C. Tramell
Typeset by Jaime Willems

Printed in the United States of America

In memory of my dear mother,
Eugenia Ouren Ulvestad Bovard
[1927–2011],
sculptress, painter, wife, and loving mother
... the most kindhearted and gentle soul I ever knew.

*"I saw the alchemy of perspective reduce my world,
and all my other life, to grains in a cup.
I learned to watch, to put my trust in other hands than mine.
And I learned to wander.
I learned what every dreaming child needs to know—
that no horizon is so far that you cannot get above it or beyond it."*

Beryl Markham
West with the Night

CONTENTS

CHAPTER 1 Racing with the Moon 1

CHAPTER 2 Gilly's Sanctuary 3

CHAPTER 3 A Far Distant Place 5

CHAPTER 4 Mean Zeke 9

CHAPTER 5 Freya and the Cats 12

CHAPTER 6 Max 17

CHAPTER 7 At the Docks 23

CHAPTER 8 The Great Escape 25

CHAPTER 9 Getting Ready for the Race 30

CHAPTER 10 Bolo's Advice 32

CHAPTER 11 The Letter 37

CHAPTER 12 The Bib 38

CHAPTER 13 Stretching the Truth 40

CHAPTER 14 Last-Minute Preparations 43

CHAPTER 15 The Night before the Race 45

CHAPTER 16 Race Morning 47

CHAPTER 17 On the Trail 51

CHAPTER 18 The First Night 52

CHAPTER 19 A Lucky Ride to Willow 55

CHAPTER 20 A Sign of Things to Come 57

CHAPTER 21 Crossing the Susitna River 59

CHAPTER 22 Wolverine 63

CHAPTER 23 The Ninth Cat 68

CHAPTER 24 Moose Attack 70

CHAPTER 25 Ukpik 75

CHAPTER 26 The Night of the Wolves 81

CHAPTER 27 Transformed 89

CHAPTER 28 The Blizzard 91

CHAPTER 29 The Wendigo 96

CHAPTER 30 Delirium 105

CHAPTER 31 Norton Bay 107

CHAPTER 32 A Tall Black Fin 114

CHAPTER 33 The White Bear 118

CHAPTER 34 West with the Night 124

CHAPTER 35 The Last Miles 126

CHAPTER 36 Nome 131

CHAPTER 37 The Journey's End 135

CHAPTER 38 Home at Last 138

EPILOGUE 143

TRIBUTE 145

ACKNOWLEDGMENTS 146

CHAPTER 1

RACING WITH THE MOON

Gilly was alone. Dark shapes moved at the edge of the woods, and the mournful howling of wolves rose into the night. Beyond the alpine snowfield, jagged ice-laden mountain peaks clawed at the raven-black sky. There was a dim glow in the distance. Was it a village or the ember of a dying fire? She knew that she had to get there, but the idea of crossing the wasteland of snow and ice that lay before her was overwhelming. A cold wind burned her eyes and cheeks, and she was numb with cold. She leaned into the fierce wind and began trudging toward the glow on the horizon. She stumbled and fell. She cried and pushed up against the hard, frozen snow.

Something brushed against her and, reaching out, Gilly buried her hand in coarse fur. She smelled the pungent odor of a wild animal, then felt the bristle of whiskers and a cold nose pressed against her cheek. She trembled and awaited the inevitable. Suddenly, large canine teeth lifted her from the ground and dropped her into a wood-frame sled. Copper eyes glowed in a wide circle around her. Before she could cry out, the sled lurched forward. She could see now that it was pulled by a clan of giant, feral beasts that surged and bounded across the frozen snowpack. Snarling and caterwauling as they ran, their roars echoed over the gusting wind.

The aurora borealis cast its wavering yellowish-green flares across the bowl of the night sky. The snow crackled under the sled's runners and Gilly could only take shallow, short breaths in the frigid air. Then, as the sled gained speed, faster, faster, it bounced and lifted from the ground, then miraculously rose into the heavens. They were racing with the moon. Wisps of cloud scudded by like the spindrift of thistledown. Wingless, they soared across the sky.

Gilly closed her eyes and opened them again. Nothing changed. Was it a dream? She felt regal and terrified all at once. She was flying across the boreal night with a team of snarling wild creatures in the traces. Bathed in moonbeams, their elongated shadows leapt eerily across the snowfield. The constellations of the zodiac wheeled across the star-cobbled path of the Milky Way. The moon guided their way like a lighthouse in the endless sea of the universe.

She knew she had crossed into the spirit world. Yet something still shadowed them, followed them. Something not of this world had their scent. She could feel it, as the native people smell a storm. Looking down she saw dark, distorted shapes racing across the barren landscape far below. Creatures with red eyes howled and snapped at the sky.

Then, suddenly, the air exploded and she was tumbling downward, falling through the sky. She didn't scream or shout. She held her amulet in her hand and prayed to the gods of snow and ice, to the great polar bear, Nanuk, and to Orca, the black-and-white whale. She started to sing the native people's Death Song, as she had been taught, but abruptly she stopped falling . . . and all was silent.

CHAPTER 2

GILLY'S SANCTUARY

When Gilly finally opened her eyes, she was lying in her own bed, safe and sound. She patted herself down. Two legs and two arms. "Whew," she muttered to herself, "what a dream!" A breeze wafted through the partially cracked window and cooled her cheek. She'd had "crazy" dreams before, so she turned over, curled up under the down comforter, and was soon peacefully asleep. Two cats lay at the foot of her bed. They mewed at each other, as cats do, but their eyes blazed strangely in the shadowed room. Lola was a gray and rust-colored tabby with a gentle disposition. Shadow was a pure black Bombay, sleek and elegant as a panther. He had one tattered ear and a scarred muzzle from his alley cat fighting days.

"A whole lot of tossin' and turnin' this night," purred Shadow. "She's truly a 'darkling child' . . . like me, eh?"

"She sees things others don't see," murmured Lola. "She wants to climb unclimbable mountains and unravel rainbows, that's all."

"Well, there are some wicked things out there that she hasn't seen yet," said Shadow.

"The heroine gets the adventure she is ready for!" Lola twitched her whiskers and wiggled her nose.

"Maybe so, but I worry about her. She's our only kiddo," he said.

"She is growing up, dear. You worry too much!"

"Well, somebody has to!" said the black cat with a flick of his tail.

The room was bathed in early-morning sunshine. Golden pillars of light spanned from the window to the floor. From the sanctum of her bed, Gilly would often watch the columns of sunlight glide across her room. In winter the days were long and dark, but in summer, there were nearly twenty hours of daylight. Her room was a place of comfort and retreat where she read, drew pictures, schemed, and imagined. It was her lair. Her desk was a door-sized slab of knotty pine that her dad had sanded smooth and mounted on birch limbs. At the back of the desk sat a low-resolution microscope and a sketchbook filled with Gilly's colorful drawings of butterflies, beetles, flowers, and winged seahorses. A stuffed great horned owl sat at the far corner of the table. On a shelf was an array of tattered books, including *The Jungle Book*, *West with the Night*, *The Golden Compass*, *Twenty Thousand Leagues Under the Sea*, *The Call of the Wild*, and *The Once and Future King*. In the corner lay a large book, Rumphius's *The Ambonese Curiosity Cabinet*, filled with intricate ink drawings of spiraling nautilus shells, Portuguese jellyfish, and nobby crustaceans. A scarlet "Tour of Anchorage" cross-country ski bib with white piping hung from the wall with a first-place ribbon attached.

"Gillian, wake up!" Dr. Kate Wells rapped on the door to her daughter's room. "Breakfast is ready. You'll be late for school." She pushed the door open and looked inside.

Gilly was still sound asleep under the pile of covers. Shadow and Lola had moved to the head of the bed to commandeer some pillow space. "The stories you'd tell, if you could talk," muttered Kate to the two basking cats. They looked at each other with wide Cheshire "I won't tell if you won't tell" grins.

Not seeing any movement from Gilly, Kate tickled her daughter's feet to rouse her. Up popped a drowsy, eye-rubbing, red-headed girl. "Was it just a dream, or an omen?" Gilly wondered. She did not notice the swatch of tawny fur that clung to her windowsill.

CHAPTER 3

A FAR DISTANT PLACE

Gilly Wells was twelve years old and lived with her parents, her two cats, and dog, Bolo, in a modest home on the outskirts of Anchorage, Alaska. America's largest and northernmost state was not far from the Arctic Circle and the top of the world as we know it. It was a beautiful, rugged wilderness with grand mountains sitting next to the sea. Although Russia sat just across the Bering Strait, if you were honest, you couldn't quite see it from the Wells house. From their porch, Gilly could watch the daily panorama of sunlight and moonbeams dancing across the elegant and temperamental Chugach mountain range.

Gilly took after her mother with her rusty hair and freckles. It was rumored that she could ski before she could walk and purred when she napped. She rarely cried, even when young, except when their first cat, Charlie, died. Then Gilly lay by the motionless creature through the night until her mother lifted her away before the backyard burial. Now she was a tomboy through and through. She could run faster than any kid in her class and could do twenty-five pull-ups. She was a top cross-country skier and won her age group in the Tour of Anchorage quarter marathon. Some of her classmates and teachers thought she had an attitude problem, but she just knew what she liked and what she didn't, and saw no reason to pretend otherwise. Not everybody liked that kind of honesty in a young lady, of course, but Gilly's parents guided her gently towards a responsible independence. "Si se puede" or "Yes, I can" was her favorite saying from Spanish class.

    Gilly's mom, Kate, was an animal doctor. She had auburn hair, green eyes, and a quick smile. Kate had strong forearms from her years working with animals. She made people laugh and they were happy to be in her presence. She had grown up on a farm in Montana, hunting and fishing. She was born a Tollefson and had gone to St. Olaf College in Minnesota. She had traveled all over Scandinavia and Europe, and then returned to America to attend vet school in Colorado. She moved to Alaska once done, and met Gil Wells when he brought one of his dogs to see the "new vet."

    Gilly's father, Gil, was a lean, rangy man. He had bright gray eyes with crow's-feet at the corners from his years outdoors in the wind and sun. He had a tousled shock of straw-colored hair that reminded one of the errant schoolboy he must have been when Gilly's age. His hands were calloused and he was missing the end of the index finger of his left hand. He had lost it in a wood splitter accident when he was sixteen years old, but he always told Gilly's friends that it was in the belly of a saltwater crocodile from his Australia wandering years.

    In fact, Gil had worn a crocodile tooth on a lanyard for many years as a good-luck piece. He claimed that the fang had protected him in the Alaskan wild because it had a magic unknown on the North American continent. He gave it to Gilly when she turned eleven and started to do longer skis into the woods. Once, in a dark part of the forest, she thought she felt it jump while hanging around her neck, but later she was sure she'd been mistaken.

    Gil now worked as a journalist and editor for the Anchorage paper. But in his twenties and thirties he had been an up-and-coming dog musher and one of the best in Alaska. He had raced the Iditarod seven times and finished in the top ten on two occasions. Once he might have won, but he stopped to help another musher and his dogs that had been attacked by a bull moose.

Gilly & the Snowcats

The Iditarod dog race was an oddity for people in the lower forty-eight states, and most of them didn't know much about it. Everyone in Alaska knew all about the Iditarod. Gilly had composed a short paper about the race for her social studies class. In it she wrote:

The Iditarod race commemorates a 1925 dogsled journey that carried the diphtheria vaccine from Nenana to Nome, Alaska, to help treat an epidemic that threatened the children of the town. Six people, mostly children, died of diphtheria at that time and many were threatened by the epidemic. The serum was carried from Anchorage to Nenana near Fairbanks by train. A total of twenty sled handlers called "mushers" and over one hundred dogs transported the precious serum in relay fashion 674 miles to Nome in 127 hours (just over five days) despite a fierce winter storm! The rescue mission captured the attention of the entire lower United States and made heroes of the mushers and their dogs. The most notable musher in the relay was Leonhard Seppala, whose lead dog named Togo led the team that carried the vaccine through ninety-one miles of the most brutal and dangerous sections of the trail. Gunnar Kaasen mushed the final team that delivered the serum to Nome. His lead dog, Balto, has a statue modeled after him, representing all the brave sled dogs, in Central Park in New York City.

The first Iditarod race from Anchorage to Nome occurred in 1973. There have been races every year since then. The name Iditarod comes from the native Ingalik word "haiditarod" which means a "far distant place." Most mushers rotate twelve to sixteen dogs over the course of the race, but there must be at least six dogs on the towline at the finish. Although most competitors are from Alaska, there are entries from all over the world. Up to seventy mushers and about 1,200 dogs usually compete every year.

Only men participated in the Iditarod in its early years, but several women have since finished first. In 1985, Libby Riddles was the first woman to win the race. Susan Butcher, who sadly died of leukemia in 2006, won the race four times after Riddles's success. Aliy Zirkle has been the top female competitor in recent years, finishing second on three separate occasions! The fastest time on record is 8 days, 13 hours, 4 minutes, and 19 seconds by

Dallas Seavey in 2014. Zirkle had the lead for part of the race and finished second by only 2 minutes and 22 seconds when she stopped to let her dogs rest from the wind!

The race is officially 1,049 miles to honor Alaska's status as the forty-ninth state. The race has a ceremonial start on the first Saturday in March from Fourth Avenue in downtown Anchorage. Mushers start based on a lottery and order of registration. The finish is on Front Street in Nome.

Gilly received an "A" on her paper!

Gil Wells had given up racing when he met Gilly's mom and started a "real job" with the local paper. He sold all his dogs except for his faithful lead dog, Bolo. Gilly had gone mushing many times with her father and his friends. She knew the names of all the famous mushers and admired the women most of all. Women like Susan Butcher, Libby Riddles, and Aliy Zirkle had all been told they wouldn't be able to keep up with the men. Instead, they had won, or at least had beaten many of the men. Someday Gilly planned to join this brave group of women on the podium. The only problem was that she liked cats.

CHAPTER 4

MEAN ZEKE

A few days after her dream, Gilly and her parents were sitting in the living room watching the start of the Iditarod race on the television. The sled dogs were yelping and milling about. The mushers, mostly bearded men, and a few women too, were getting ready to go. And then, they were off!

A big musher named Zeke Meaner, nicknamed "Mean Zeke" for his surly temperament, surged into the lead. Mean Zeke had a thick black thatch of hair and a beard to match. He had a crooked nose with a long scar on his right cheek where a dog had bitten him, earning it an early grave. His eyes were dark and piercing, more animal than human. He had an evil smile and a black heart. That the Iditarod race was run during the darkness of winter suited him well, for it concealed his foul intentions and cruel behavior. He seemed to enjoy making animals, and people, suffer whenever the opportunity arose. He was belligerence personified.

Zeke had a stormy relationship with the race organizers. He was hard on his dogs; harder than most people thought was right. He rarely talked in a normal voice. He bellowed and yelled at everyone. He was bluster and swagger, but at 6'2" and 200 pounds, he was an intimidating presence. Most mushers were lithe men and women, and Zeke was a brute among them. He bullied his opponents at every occasion. He had been penalized for whipping a dog, and once

broke an opponent's arm in a tightly contested race, leaving the man injured by the trail.

Gil Wells was one of the few men who had ever stood up to Mean Zeke. He'd confronted Zeke once when Zeke was lashing a dog at the start, and received an unexpected blow in retaliation. Gil, who was a solid 185 pounds, had knocked Zeke down in the ensuing fight, but the race officials had pulled them apart before any blood was spilled. There was no love lost between the two men; that was certain.

CHAPTER 5

FREYA AND THE CATS

Sitting in front of the television, Gilly said defiantly, "Someday I am going to do the Iditarod." She was an excellent student who always got her homework done early, but she had an adventurer's spirit.

"How are you going to do the race with no dogs?" said her father, looking up over his newspaper through his reading glasses.

"I dunno. Get some, I guess. It's too bad you didn't keep your huskies."

"Pretty expensive to board a team of Siberians," he said. "Besides, they would be just as old as Bolo now, sixteen. He was six when he was in his prime. It's a young animal's game."

Bolo had been a savvy and devoted lead dog for Gil for nearly five years. He was nearly blind now, and limped about slowly on his arthritic hips. He was grizzled but still yelped devotedly and smiled a toothy grin to see his master coming home. He had a big cushion next to Gil's reading chair and sometimes rested in the barn in the soft straw.

Suddenly, inspired by her dream, Gilly said, "What if I don't use dogs? What if I use a different animal?"

Gil Wells looked at his daughter curiously. Then, putting his paper down, with his glasses at the very end of his nose, he said, "Well, Gilly, there have been a number of attempts to use other animals to pull sleds. Horses, goats, and domesticated caribou, or reindeer, have all been tried without much success."

Bolo looked up and nodded as if saying, "Yup, yup, very true!"

"What animal do you propose to hitch to your sled?" asked Gil.

"Cats!" she said triumphantly.

"Cats?" he said.

"Cats!" she repeated.

"That," he mused, "is the most improbable thing I have ever heard of in my life!" And he started to laugh, first in chuckles, then in rolling waves of laughter, tears running down his cheeks.

Gilly's mom came into the TV room to see what was the matter. She had an "Ok, spill the beans" look on her face. Gil was wiping tears from his cheek. "I'm sorry, honey," he said to Gilly, "I'm not making fun of you. It's just the most quizzical thing I have ever imagined." Then to his wife, "Gilly proposes running the Iditarod with a cat-drawn sled rather than using a traditional team of dogs."

"Well, I don't see what is so odd about that, dear," Kate said to her husband. "She will just need some well-trained and very fit cats. Besides, felines have long been regarded as royalty in some societies, sitting on the throne with emperors, while the dogs groveled for scraps at the foot of the table. The god of wine, Bacchus, had a chariot drawn by a pair of cheetahs. In fact, in the Scandinavian cultures, the goddess Freya was pulled in her chariot by none other than two giant cats named Bygul and Trigul. Did you know that, Gilly? How about you, Mr. Smarty Pants?"

"I did not know that," admitted Gil. "Gimme some particulars."

Gilly's mom walked into the study and looked at a row of books. Shelves of novels and texts extended from the floor to the ceiling; the Wells family liked to read. Kate pulled a book of

Scandinavian mythology from the shelf. She scanned the index and flipped the pages. "Here we go!" she said, and laid the book open before them.

The illustration showed the goddess Freya as an imposing figure. She was tall and regal with a long gown that flowed behind her off the back of the chariot. She had torrents of hair and blazing eyes. She stood in the chariot with two oversized, powerful, and sinewy cats harnessed to the front of the chariot.

"There is even a Swedish stamp commemorating her with a cat-drawn chariot," said Kate. "Look!"

"Wow!" said Gilly, suddenly affirmed and buoyant in her hair-brained scheme. She gave her dad a "don't mess with me" glare. "Cats are smarter than dogs," she declared. "They are probably stronger pound for pound and have great endurance!"

A chastened Mr. Wells, the experienced ex-musher and Iditarod finisher, said, "Ok, if you two can spin some scientific formula and transmogrify a mob of cats into a formidable team, you have my complete and total blessing! All I know is that I don't think I'd like to be out on the trail with Lola and Shadow and have Mean Zeke and a howling harness of huskies bearing down on me, that's all I'm sayin. Maybe check with the zoo to see if they will loan you a few cheetahs, or maybe some lions and tigers," he added with a wry grin.

Gilly scowled at him and his wife looked exasperated. He threw his hands up in a gesture of defeat. He smiled sheepishly at his daughter and winked at his wife, an act that was not unnoticed by Gilly.

Mr. Wells got up and went into the kitchen to fix the evening dinner. Kate put her hand on her daughter's shoulder. "How many cats do you think you will need for this enterprise, honey?"

"About nine," said Gilly. "A lead cat and four pairs in the traces. Besides, cats have nine lives, so it's an omen, isn't it?"

"Perhaps. And will Lola and Shadow be part of the team?"

"Of course. They have already told me, more or less, that they want to go. They are increasing their training by chasing more mice in the barn," she fibbed. The Wells family had an old barn on the back of their acreage where Gil had previously housed his dog team. Now it served mostly as a toolshed for yard equipment and woodworking.

"They are looking quite fit," observed her mother. "Hmm," she thought to herself. "Will wonders never cease?"

"Well," said Kate, "although dogs have been faithful companions to humans for centuries, there never was a dog who could equal the great cats in size, ferocity, or elegance. I still have days in clinic where I am more terrified of an irascible old tomcat than the orneriest rottweiler," Kate laughed.

"You know, dear, the old expression 'tougher than herding cats' is meant to suggest that cats have a very independent nature. Which isn't all bad," she said with a smile as she smoothed Gilly's hair. "But for that unique individual, be it Freya or Bacchus or a stubborn red-haired girl, gaining the allegiance and command of a team of great cats would be a thing of incredible grace and beauty. It is a worthy dream."

"Thanks, Mom," said Gilly.

"For what?"

"For understanding, for not treating me like a little kid . . . and for letting me dream."

"That's what moms are for," Kate said with a smile.

"Spaghetti is served," yelled Gil from the kitchen.

"*Bon appetit!*" said Mom.

"*Me gusto*," said Gilly, using the Spanish she had been studying at the international immersion school for nearly five years now.

Later, Dr. Wells said to her husband, "We need to encourage her creative side, dear. What a novel idea: a team of cats. What will that girl think up next? With that kind of imagination, she can be a famous writer and not have to study chemistry or spend a decade in graduate school or do a residency. It'll save us a bundle in tuition, eh?" she said with a conspiratorial smile.

"Before I forget, dear, remember that we will be in Australia next March. We need to confirm our flights to Brisbane and make sure that Aunt Sally can stay with Gilly, so there are no snafus. We need to make sure we have everything booked early for our anniversary vacation."

"It will be the first time in over twenty years that I will miss the start of the Iditarod," said Gil, shaking his head. "I can't believe it has been fifteen years since we got married. Total bliss the whole time, of course." He winked at his wife. Gil liked to wink.

CHAPTER 6

MAX

The next morning, Gilly was up early in the barn digging through the storage. Soon she emerged with a scaled-down version of a dog sled that her father had made for her a few years earlier. It was built from rugged ash with solid hardwood runners. Gilly had diligently hand-sewn a set of leather harnesses for the two cats. She whistled for her faithful kitties. Lola and Shadow soon ambled into the barn.

"Ok," said Gilly, "so let's try pulling this sled and see how it goes."

Lola and Shadow looked at each other with raised eyebrows. "What?"

Although her parents had patiently suffered through her claims of talking with her cats, Gilly had always communicated in the cat tongue that other humans couldn't hear. It was a gift that she had discovered in early childhood. The soft mews, purrs, and yowls were a unique and distinct language, just like any other, when one listened carefully enough.

"Can you just try pulling the sled?" asked Gilly softly. "Dad and Mom don't really think that a team of cats can pull a sled and run the Iditarod. I told them you could."

"You did what?" asked Shadow incredulously.

"I said we, well, you . . . and a full team of cats, of course, could pull a sled in the Iditarod."

"Of course," said Shadow, with only a hint of sarcasm. "And where do we get this team of cats?"

"Fate will provide!" said Gilly, reciting a quote she had heard one of her parents say at one time or another. "Please, let's just try," implored Gilly, "otherwise I will feel like a complete and utter fool."

"Damned if we do and damned if we don't," muttered Shadow to Lola under his breath. "Let's just humor the kid, eh?"

He jumped up on a bale of hay facing Gilly at eye level as she knelt down to work on the sled harness. "Ok, Gilly, we'll give it a try. We're game. Partners to the end and all that. Now, what do you want us to do?"

Gilly smiled broadly and hugged them both. "I knew you'd help me," she said with an exalted grin. "Here, step into the leather traces. I'll harness you into the towline and we can do our first test run."

The two cats obediently allowed themselves to be strapped into the leather traces. Then, with tentative steps, they began to pull the sled about the barn floor. They were solid, muscular cats who were fit from five years of barn hunting and life in the rugged outdoors of Alaska. Gilly walked behind the sled as they emerged from the barn and out into the back meadow. They were a curious spectacle.

Unbeknownst to the three, they were being observed by a pair of eyes from the back hedgerow. A dark nose sniffed the air, picked up the scent of two cats and a single human, and watched as the odd contraption drew closer.

The watcher was downwind and had little chance of being detected as long as he remained silent. Closer they came. When they were about twenty feet away, he could control himself no longer. "Good lord Effie! What in the world are you doing?"

Both Lola and Shadow jumped into the air, embarrassed

to have been surprised and caught unawares. Gilly defensively got between her cats and the strange voice. "Show yourself," she said bravely.

Slowly the bushes parted, and the golden, furry face of a grizzled but friendly Maine coon cat emerged. As was typical of his breed, he was far bigger than a normal domestic cat, weighing well over twenty pounds. He carried his tail at an odd angle; it had clearly been broken at some point in his seven years.

"Who are you?" asked Gilly, eyeing the prodigious feline warily.

"Name is Max," said the Maine coon.

"What do you want?"

"Nothin'. Just traveling through on my way south. I guess some would say I am a 'feral' cat. I go where I want and I do what I want. I don't bother nobody and hopefully nobody bothers me. I usually hug the rail lines and jump a train now and again as my mood suits. This seemed like a nice pasture for a nap. And it was, till I was disturbed by two fellow felines and a young whelp traipsing about pulling a dog sled. Dangdest thing I have ever seen, if I do say so myself."

"We are in training," said Gilly. "We are going to run the Iditarod."

Max half snorted and his eyes grew wide. "You gotta be kiddin'." Then to the two cats, he said, "You agreed to this?"

Lola looked at Shadow and Shadow looked at Lola. Neither wanted to speak first.

Finally Max broke the silence. "Is this a team of mute, deaf, and dumb felines, or what? Cat got yer tongue? Ha ha ha!" He had a booming, infectious laugh.

"Look," said Lola, addressing the gangly lout, "we are helping Miss Gilly, our very kind master, who speaks cat fluently as you may have noticed, to pursue her goal of competing in the Iditarod. She

Gilly & the Snowcats

is an aspiring musher and a visionary among humans!"

Realizing the providential nature of the encounter, Gilly blurted, "Why don't you join us? We are recruiting right now! Holy cow . . . three down and only six to go! I need to make a longer gang line and add a harness!" And before he could refuse, Max had become a member of the Gilly Wells cat-sled team. His wandering days were over and his destiny now lay before him.

Later, Shadow, Lola, and Max were lazing about in the barn chatting, or as they say, "catting," and getting better acquainted. With a sudden mewl, Shadow, who was a bit of a skeptic by nature, said, "Talk about thinking outside the box! This kid is a hoot. But do we really want to encourage the girl with this crazy idea?"

"Who says it's crazy?" asked Lola. "I rather think it's an interesting proposition. If Bolo could do it, we can do it too."

"Lola, be reasonable. Old Bolo may be crippled and nearly blind now, but in his prime, Bolo was one tough Siberian. We can't challenge packs of huskies in a thousand-mile race across the Alaskan wilderness. It's freezing, the snow is deep, there are icy rivers, belligerent moose, hungry wolves, snowstorms, and hallucinations. You've heard the stories!"

"So?"

"We might get killed!"

"We might, but remember, we do have nine lives. We're cats after all."

"Exactly my point," said Shadow. "We are cats, not huskies!"

"Dear," said Lola, "I think your dreams are too small. It is our very feline nature to do the opposite of what we are expected to do."

"Not to intrude, but I tend to agree," said Max diplomatically.

"In the end, it's all about toughness, determination, and luck," said Lola.

"Easier said than done," muttered Shadow. "Maybe we should

wander down to the docks and see if there are any strays hunting for wharf rats. They'd be tough enough for this job."

"Good idea," purred Max. "I've seen a few scruffy, rough-and-tumble characters on the outskirts of town, and the shipping lines often attract the 'on the road' types."

"The thing is," added Lola, "the race entry deadline closes in two weeks. Gilly is using her newspaper-route money for the entry fee and entering under her father's name. There is no time to lose!"

CHAPTER 7

AT THE DOCKS

The next day, Lola, Shadow, and Max slipped out the back of the barn and headed out to make their daily reconnaissance of the neighborhood. Satisfied that all was well, they headed down toward the harbor. Soon they were sauntering along the docks where freighters and seagoing vessels loaded and unloaded. A large shipping freighter had just docked that morning and lay moored along the pier. They stopped to gaze up at the rusted sides of the iron hulk.

"Psst! Hey, you cats!" Lola, Max, and Shadow looked toward the sound that emerged from behind a large shipping crate stamped with the label "Smirnov." A large mottled Himalayan cat, with eyes like black opals, peeked from behind the wooden box.

"What do you want?" said Max.

"I need help!" implored the Himalayan. "My friend Ravi and I smuggled aboard the *Samovar* two weeks ago in Russia, and arrived dis morning. I am from de Himalayas and Ravi is from Siberia. Dockworkers caught Ravi this morning and dey took him to animal shelter. We have to get him back!" she said. "You have to help me."

"Hmmm," said Lola. "Is Ravi pretty strong?"

"Why yes. He is strong like tiger. Siberian tiger is in his blood."

"Curiouser and curiouser!" said Shadow.

"What is your name?" asked Lola.

"I am Sasha."

"Welcome to Anchorage, Alaska, Sasha. We call it Anchor Town. I'm Lola. This is Shadow and this is Max. Let's go see if we can spring Ravi."

"'Spring'?"

"Get him out of the animal shelter."

"Yes, bery good!" said Sasha, filled with hope inspired by her new friends.

CHAPTER 8

THE GREAT ESCAPE

Back at the barn, Lola and the cats explained Sasha and Ravi's predicament to Gilly. She listened thoughtfully.

"Ok, here is what we do," said Gilly. "I distract the clerk up front, you run through, creating a diversion, and in the confusion I will slip in back and free Ravi from his cage. But we will have to be fast. What does Ravi look like?"

Sasha looked worried. "He big cat. Mostly orange with black stripes. Heart of gold," she added. "Eyes like coal."

"Ok, I'm ready," said Gilly. "Let's go!"

Outside the Anchorage Animal Shelter was a sign that read: *Impounded Animals Unclaimed after 5 Days Will Be Euthanized.*

"Did you read that?" said Gilly.

"Yes," gulped Lola, Shadow, and Max in unison. The three barn cats hid with Sasha in the bushes just outside the entry door.

Gilly pushed open the heavy metal door of the shelter. It smelled strongly of antiseptic. There were waxed linoleum floors and bright overhead lights. Behind a high counter stood a grumpy-looking man with black glasses. He had a droopy moustache, a pale complexion, and a tired face.

"What can I do for you, young lady?" He looked down at her through horn-rimmed glasses.

"I lost my cat this morning," said Gilly. "He is orange with black stripes."

"Yeah, we found a cat looks like that, no tags or collar. We thought it came off the Russian freighter the *Samovar*. One of your parents with you?"

"No," said Gilly in frustration.

"Well, we can't release no animals to no one under eighteen. It's just the rules."

Gilly started to shout, "I want my cat! I want my cat!" at the top of her lungs. Then she opened the main door so that Lola, Shadow, Max, and Sasha ran into the lobby snarling and hissing. The clerk ran out from behind the counter muttering and stumbling to try to catch the darting cats. While he was distracted, Gilly slipped behind the counter into the holding area where the kennels were housed. A motley array of dogs and cats of all sizes, shapes, and colors stared at her expectantly from behind their bars. A cacophony of howls and yowls arose as she ran down the aisle looking for a cat she didn't know. She quickly scanned the cages. Finally, in the back cage, she saw a flash of orange-and-black stripes and dark piercing eyes.

"Are you Ravi?" she yelled.

Ravi's eyes widened in surprise. Who in this foreign land knew his name, let alone a girl human speaking cat? He came to the front of the cage as the young red-haired girl flipped open the latch. Instinctively, he shrank back in the cage and snarled.

"Come on, Ravi," Gilly urged. "We don't have much time. Sasha sent us! We gotta get out of here pronto!"

She reached into his cage and he jumped into her arms. He smelled like sea salt and musty ropes. Gilly held him tightly and ran for the door.

As she was nearing the exit, she saw a row of cages marked with a sign: DAY FIVE: UNCLAIMED. Gilly gasped. "No!" Without thinking, she flipped open the latches and swung the cage doors wide open.

As she was turning to run, three rough-looking cats caught her eye. They had a haughty demeanor and looked out of their cages at her with regal impertinence. "Do you like to run?" she shouted at them in cat lingo.

"Oh yeah, baby," purred the golden Savannah.

"Si!" said the powerful multicolor.

"Like lightning," hissed the sleek Serengeti cat.

"Well, come on with us then!" shouted Gilly.

To add chaos to the confusion, she ran along the row of cages, tugging down the latches to release as many other cats and dogs as she could. A boisterous howling, screeching, and barking riot of furry animals ensued as black, white, tan, spotted, and striped canines and felines tumbled onto the floor. Soon there were some twenty cats and dogs careening about the room in a freewheeling melee. Gilly pushed open the door and darted past the bewildered clerk. She had Ravi in her arms and the other three cats were right behind her and outside in seconds. The clerk had no option but to address the howling chaos in the back room, and the escapee cats were quickly forgotten.

Gilly and her entourage of cats reassembled at the barn. Sasha and Ravi were happily reunited. Ravi was a rugged vibrant fellow. He kept asking Sasha incredulously, "How you do this?"

And Sasha just kept saying, "The girl speak our language and her friends are our friends now!"

Meanwhile, the other three cats were spilling their stories. The Savannah cat was named Jamila. She had a big scar across her muzzle from a fight with a mongrel hound. "Ya mon," she said, "my claws still work real good." She had been with a military family for several years. Then she had been abandoned on the Alaska-Canadian Highway and picked up outside of Anchorage by another family who left her at the shelter when they headed back south. She had relatives on the west coast of Africa. She

could climb a tree faster than a coconut fell to earth.

The multicolor was named Garcia. He went by Gar. He had circular dark rings on his coat like a young rainforest jaguar. He had lived most of his life in Colombia and Brazil before sailing up the west coast to Alaska with a family transporting a boat for a friend. Gar had a big boxy head, a barrel chest, and a predator's powerful jaws. Despite his appearance, he had a gentle soul . . . until provoked, and then look out.

The yellow Serengeti cat was named Che. He was lean and rangy in appearance. Where Gar exuded power, Che was the epitome of speed. He just looked fast. When he walked, he sauntered. When he ran, he blazed. He used to drive dogs mad by darting into their territory and outrunning them to trees where he sat taunting them.

Gilly proudly assessed her sled team. Suddenly they had gone from the original two of Lola and Shadow to three with the addition of Max. Then Sasha and Ravi came on board and made five. Now, unexpectedly, from the animal shelter, came Jamila, Gar, and Che so that they were now eight! Gilly had her team. Ideally she would have liked a ninth cat to pull lead, but she was overjoyed to have the eight stalwarts before her.

CHAPTER 9

GETTING READY FOR THE RACE

Every day Gilly left kibble and water out for sustenance. Every day she sneaked extra scraps of food and used some of her paper-route money to buy additional cat food full of protein and supplements. Every day she walked down to the nearby cannery and lugged home a bucket of fish trimmings. She needed to help her team put on muscle and strength. There wasn't a mouse or a rat to be seen anywhere near the Wells property.

Over the ensuing months, through the fall and early winter, they practiced pulling on the centerline of the sled daily. She had reinforced the small sled with supports from one of her dad's old frames. Gilly clipped in individual harness traces and towlines for each of the four pairs of cats. She sewed comfortable, softly padded harnesses custom fitted for each feline. Gilly was adept at using the heavy-duty family sewing machine for sewing canvas packs, webbing, and leather straps. Some points she reinforced with a hand awl. A tailor couldn't have done a better job.

One bright fall afternoon, when the white bark of the aspen trees contrasted with the golden leaves and the sky was bluer than a bluebird, Gilly assembled her team. Max, as a Maine coon, was by far the largest cat, and Ravi, a Siberian, was the next largest at seventeen pounds. Gilly paired them at the rear of the centerline at the "wheel" position. They were the brutes, the power generators of the team, and would do the lion's share of the pulling, so to speak. Gar was paired with Shadow. Sasha, the Himalayan, was paired with Lola. Sharing the lead was the faster and lighter pair of Jamila and Che, both lean and whippet fast. It wasn't a perfect balance but it was close. Gilly eyed her team with glowing admiration.

One by one the cats fell into the rhythm of pulling the sled. By the time the first snow had settled on the ground, the cats had developed a playful camaraderie and enthusiasm for the challenge. Even in the dry season they could pull the sled easily across the grassy meadow at a good clip. With the early snowfall, the mechanical advantage of runners on snow made Gilly's weight seem almost inconsequential. Their confidence was growing, but there were still some doubts.

CHAPTER 10

BOLO'S ADVICE

One night after Gilly had gone into the house for dinner, Gar approached old Bolo who lay resting in the hay. Bolo had enjoyed listening to the cats run, pull the sled, and train, but knew they had no idea what they were getting themselves into. Despite people's belief that cats and dogs got along like oil and water, Bolo, Shadow, and Lola had been friends since the first day they met. Bolo liked all the new cats as well.

"So, Bolo, tell us what it's really like to run the Iditarod," implored Max. The other cats gathered around the old Siberian, sitting on bales of hay or lying on the ground in a semicircle before him.

Bolo lifted his head from his brindle-colored paws. "Do you want the sugar-coated version or can you handle the truth?" he asked, looking out over them through his opaque, rheumy eyes. His lips curled over his worn canines in a whimsical, knowing smile.

"Give it to us straight!" said Che, lounging on a hay bale.

"Ok," said Bolo. "It's a cold, windy, snowy, desolate, unforgiving place. The real wilderness. I know you guys are tough. Failure isn't the problem. Death is the problem. It's a genuine possibility for an experienced and highly trained dog team. For a team of cats, I'd say it's a high probability. In the Iditarod, it's not a question of *if* something bad will happen, it's *when*. You are a mix of breeds and temperaments. How will you get along on the trail in a crisis? When a moose attacks? What then?"

"Ok," said Gar, "so there are some cons. What about the pros?"

Bolo stared at them, unseeing. "It's good exercise and you get to see rural Alaska, a thousand miles of it, mostly at night. How's that for a positive? Negatives? Hmm. How about hunger, mind-numbing cold, brutal wind, wild beasts, pain, Norton Bay, Mean Zeke . . . I could go on.

"Remember, there are only six daylight hours in March, so you run in darkness most of the time. Then again, you felines have pretty good night vision. But Gilly doesn't, so you have to see for her, guide her. You rely heavily on all your other senses: smell, sound, touch, taste. Sometimes there is moonlight, if the wind doesn't pull the clouds over the sky. I imagine it gets dark in your jungles of South America, beneath a heavy canopy of an Amazon rainforest, or in the thickets on the African veldt. But you don't have to worry about staying warm down south.

"The course looks easy enough on a human map, eh? You just go from here to there. Easy, eh? But now you are in a whiteout blizzard with fifty-mile-per-hour winds and the temperature has dropped to fifty degrees below zero. You will die if you quit moving, and you use precious energy when you move. But you have a race to run. A goal to reach. A master to serve and preserve. Maybe a life to save? The snow may be deeper than a man's waist and yet you must go through it. A howling demon wind drives the snow like needles into your face and your eyes can literally freeze. Your lungs fill with ice. The wind is a raging monster that can lift a sled and a whole team of dogs into the air and off a cliff. A team of cats might literally go into orbit!"

The cats looked downcast and uncertain. Doubts were rising.

"Yes," said Bolo, "it's no picnic, that's fer sure. I learned to find my way by relying on my instinct and trusting in ancient rhythms."

"Yet you did the race five times," said Shadow.

"Yup," said Bolo. "And loved every minute of it."

"What?" said Jamila. "I'm confused. In spite of the wind, the cold, the hunger, the pain?"

"Oh yes, and I would do it again if these old hips could carry me, and if I weren't just a blind old dog trying to predict the future."

"Vhy?" said Sasha.

"Because it defined my life, and it gave our team and Gilly's father a reason to be alive. You are tested and challenged in a way normal life cannot test you. Your heart is pounding in your chest, the blood pulsing in your veins, every muscle and nerve firing in perfect harmony as you draw the sled across the endless landscape. And if you bring your master home safely, then you can hold your head up to the end of your days. You can know you did something truly grand."

"But you are saying *we* shouldn't go, right?" said Jamila.

"You have to go. Why do you think you are all here?"

"Even though we're inexperienced, it's painful, and dangerous, and we could all get killed," said Che.

"Right."

"But we should *still* go?"

"Of course! You asked me to tell you about the race. I am. If you had just asked me at the beginning whether you should go with Gilly it would have saved us time." He smiled and lifted his muzzle into the air as if seeking a distant scent.

"Risking *our* lives is one thing, Bolo, but I worry about Gilly," said Lola. "How can we protect her? If something were to happen to her . . ."

Bolo looked up at his old friend and housemate. "We best protect the ones we love by giving them the courage to follow their dreams. I've known Gilly since she was a wee pink babe wriggling on the floor like any pup or kit in a litter. She is approaching a crossroads in her life. Will she pursue her dreams or abandon them as crazy, hair-brained schemes, as so many do? The gods will protect you or they will call you home. Either is better than to have stayed forever in a safe harbor when you were a beautiful vessel made to sail, a superbly designed animal made to run, or whatever it is you were meant to do. You must do that thing, you see?"

"I still don't know if this is the right thing for us to do," said Shadow, "but I think we are committed to this race. Gilly needs us."

"Wise Bolo, will you give us your blessing?" said Max.

"I will give you better than that," replied the old dog. "I will give you yourselves. Gilly couldn't have a nobler team. There is a chance you won't make it," he admitted. "In fact, I rather think you won't. But you have to try!" There was silence from the circle of cats.

"I'll get the kid next door or old Mrs. Smith to feed me while you are gone. They both like the company. Now will you felines allow an old mongrel to go gnaw on a bone and dream about ancient times on a soft cushion by the fire?"

"Good night, you mangy old cur," said Shadow. "Sleep well."

"And you," said Bolo. As he limped from the barn he turned, nodded at each cat in turn, as if in a benediction, and walked out the barn door into a starlit night that he remembered but could barely see. He scratched on the door and Gil Wells let the old dog into the house, where the warmth of the fireplace and a bowl of food were waiting.

CHAPTER 11

THE LETTER

A few weeks later, Gilly received the letter in the mail for which she had long been waiting. It was from the Iditarod committee.

Dear Gil Wells,

> *We are pleased to welcome you back to the Iditarod race. Your entry has been accepted. Although it has been over ten years since you last participated, we hope you will find the same enthusiasm in our volunteers and the same healthy competitiveness in our mushers. Oddly, your birthdate was smeared, so we have corrected it to what we have on record. Please remember that registration and bib pickup is held the Friday before the ceremonial start on Saturday. Good luck!*

Sincerely,

The Iditarod Committee

Gilly shared the letter with the team that afternoon in the barn. Her eyes glowed with a new fire and the conviction that yes, they would indeed join in this great Iditarod race.

CHAPTER 12

THE BIB

On the day before the race, Gilly walked to the Iditarod expo and bib pickup. There were displays and exhibits of sled dog harnesses, sleds, dog food, veterinary concerns, training manuals, and everything canine. There were also sponsors from pickup truck companies, power tools, and other manly things. Gilly, her heart pounding, walked to the registration table. A matronly woman with silver-blue hair sat peering at the comings and goings with a bemused smile. "Such chaos, and all for a dog race," she mused to herself. Her husband was one of the new race officials, and she had been enlisted to hand out bibs to the entrants. She was new to Alaska, accompanying a newly retired husband who had vowed to fish and hunt himself into the grave. Handing out bibs was an important but not especially glamorous job.

"Excuse me, ma'am," said Gilly.

"Yes, can I help you?" said the lady, curious as to what the young urchin was doing at this testosterone-laden event.

"Well, I am here to pick up a bib." She slid the registration letter forward across the table to the lady.

"So who and where is this Gil Wells?" said the lady. She looked up over her spectacles. "Entrants are supposed to claim their bib in person."

Gilly started to speak when she, age twelve, remembered

that she had to impersonate her father, age forty-two, to gain her entry bib. "It's for my dad," she said.

"And where is your father?"

"Well, see, I, I mean, we know you are supposed to register in person, but my dad works for the paper and he had an emergency deadline, so he dropped me off here to pick up his bib for him. He's done the race before, and he said that since he knows Buck Crawford, the organizer, it wouldn't be a problem."

"Hmmm," the lady muttered in a nasal twang. "Highly unusual."

However, the lady, who had been condescendingly stuffy before, recognized the name of the race director, and not knowing who else of import she might be offending, realized that she didn't need to make her husband any enemies this early in his time in Alaska. "Well," she said, "if your father is well known and there are extenuating circumstances, I guess we can make an exception."

As she was looking at the release-of-liability form with its feminine signature, she had a moment's doubt. Then she pushed the musher's bib, with red trim around a white panel, and the sled number #66, across the table to the girl. Upside down, which is the way Gilly read it, her bib appeared to be #99. Nine lives and a team of nine, including herself. It was a very good omen!

"Thanks, lady," said Gilly, and she bolted out of the auditorium without looking back.

CHAPTER 13

STRETCHING THE TRUTH

When Gilly returned home from the registration, her mother was working in her study. She was editing a book on animal physiology and had been quite preoccupied lately. Illustrations of horses, dogs, cats, and ferrets were neatly arrayed on her desk.

"Hi, Mom," said Gilly.

Her mother looked up. "Hi, dear. Where have you been?"

"Oh, just up at the Iditarod registration picking up my entry bib."

"What?" her mother exclaimed, putting down her laptop.

"See?" said Gilly, holding up her bib.

Her mother inhaled a gasp, and then started to laugh. "You scamp. You had me going there for a few seconds. Your sewing skills are pretty impressive. That looks very authentic. Doesn't your father have enough of those old entry bibs without your wanting your own?"

"But those are his and this is mine," replied Gilly defensively.

"Remember, your father and I are leaving early tomorrow morning for our trip to Australia. Your Aunt Sally and Uncle Joe will be staying here while we're gone."

"Perfect. Purrfect," whispered Gilly under her breath.

"What, dear?"

"Oh, I'm just thinking how much I will miss you both, Mom," said Gilly.

"We will miss you too. But the time will go quickly. We will take you to Australia with us next time. What are you planning to do this weekend?"

"Well," said Gilly, "the Iditarod starts tomorrow morning. We'll be at the start. I have entered the first cat-sled team in history."

"And do the organizers know this?" Gilly's mother really did appreciate her daughter's creative imagination. Gilly had always had play friends, spoke with her feline pets in a secret "cat" language, and conjured up elaborate scenarios for her own entertainment.

"Not yet. But when they see us they will!"

"And how long will you be gone?" inquired Kate.

"As long as it takes to git 'er done," Gilly proclaimed. Her father used this expression as a way to encourage people to stay committed to their projects until the work was finished.

"Well, I guess we will see you when we see you then, huh?"

"Yup."

"You packed warm clothes, your heavy parka, mitts, your Sorels, emergency kit, and food?"

"Of course."

"Well, you are your father's daughter . . . but I dare say you get some of that *hutzpah* from me."

"What's *hutzpah*?"

"Being feisty and grabbing for the gusto in life. Ok, enough teasing. I'm sorry we won't be able to go to the start of the race with you tomorrow. I have to go pack and get ready for the trip."

That afternoon, Gilly called her Aunt Sally, her favorite aunt, who lived up near Talkeetna in a log cabin. Aunt Sally was a free spirit who didn't like modern technology and really didn't like coming to the "big city." Uncle Joe wrote books about human potential and the pursuit of authenticity.

"Hi, Aunt Sal. This is Gilly. Say, we've had a change of plans, so you don't need to come all the way down to Anchorage. But we will still see you for the summer solstice party as planned. Okay? Yup, love you too! Bye!"

CHAPTER 14

LAST-MINUTE PREPARATIONS

Later in the afternoon, Gilly ran out to the barn. "It's only a little stretching of the truth," she muttered to herself. "Oh, what have I done?" Once she was in the barn, she called all the cats to assemble for a meeting. It was difficult to rouse them from their afternoon siesta. They were lolling about on the warm straw, basking in beams of midday sunshine. The cats raised a sleepy head from cradling paws to yawn and blink their great amber, green, or opal eyes.

"I think we should do a final practice run," said Gilly. All the cats groaned.

"Not again," muttered Gar. "Besides, it's naptime."

"It always seems to be naptime around here," barked Gilly.

"We are saving our energy for when we really need it," added Jamila. "Ya can't run down a gazelle if you're tired when you start the chase."

"Who's chasing gazelles? This is Alaska. We are pulling a sled through the Alaskan wilderness starting tomorrow!"

"True enough, true enough," replied Jami. "Just making an analogy. You know what I mean?"

"No problemo," Gilly smiled. "I am just nervous. Look at this! We have the entry bib and the sled number." She held up bib #66, then turned it upside down to become #99. "I think we were one of the last teams that entered. Isn't it fitting that cats have nine lives and we are number ninety-nine? Anyway, we are set! This is it! Tomorrow morning at nine, we will start the Iditarod!"

Che lifted his head from his paws. Softly he muttered, "I don't know about the rest of you, but I don't have nine lives left. Used up a few of them already. I hope we don't need to use too many on this wild and woolly scheme."

Gilly had walked up behind. "You don't have to come with us if you don't want to, Che."

"Na, na, sweet pea, I'm just mutterin' and talkin' stuff. You saved us from certain doom at the Animal Bin. You have sheltered us and fed us. We owe you. It is the least we can do." The other cats all nodded in agreement. "But you have to admit it is a very unorthodox thing you are proposing we do."

"Don't worry, Gilly, we are with you all the way," said Lola. Shadow nodded in agreement.

"Us too," said Ravi and Sasha in unison.

The cats formed a circle around Gilly. "You helped us and saved us, and we will run to the ends of the earth for you!" snarled Ravi. All the cats sprang into the air as if high on catnip and yowled into the darkening afternoon sky.

CHAPTER 15

THE NIGHT BEFORE THE RACE

That night at the dinner table, before Gilly's parents left to catch their flight in the early morning, they had a final dinner. Gil Wells had made his famous spaghetti and meatballs.

"So I am leaving for Nome tomorrow with the cats!" said Gilly matter-of-factly.

"Right," said her father with a knowing smile. "Call us when you get there." Kate kicked Gil under the table.

"You know, Gilly, racing sled dogs are admittedly smaller than most huskies or malamutes, but faster and with boundless endurance. How in the world could those scrawny stray cats you've been harboring in the barn compete with a prime dog team?"

It was a rhetorical question and he didn't wait for an answer. "I admit they've added some meat since you rescued them, and I haven't seen a mouse or a rat since they moved in, but the physics just doesn't work!"

"Dad," answered Gilly with tears in her eyes, "we have been practicing. You know I'm one of the top cross-country ski racers in my age group. I am a good runner and won't need to sit in the sled much. Once in motion, the coefficient of friction of the runners on snow will let us glide!"

"Coefficient of friction! Where did you come up with that?" Gil laughed.

"From you!" she said. "It was in one of the articles you wrote for *Musher Magazine*."

Kate Wells frowned. She whispered to her husband, behind her hand, "You don't think she might be serious?"

"No way," he whispered back. "Childish bravado! She's been reading too much *Tom Swift and His Diving Seacopter* . . . or maybe it was the Jules Verne or Kipling. Darn good imagination though. Does she get that from you or from me?"

"I am a scientist committed to hard data. You are the raving dreamer and schemer. So it would be from you."

"Ah, I feared as much," said Gil. He looked admiringly at his wife and then at the spitfire at the other end of the table. "Double trouble," he thought to himself, but was wise enough to stay silent.

"Ok, Gilly, will you clean up and do the dishes while we finish packing?"

When he returned, the kitchen was spotless. Gilly was in her room reading.

He poked his head into her room. "Your mom and I leave at four thirty in the morning. You called Aunt Sally, right, to remind her of our plans? She and Uncle Joe should be here mid-morning. She's a little scatterbrained sometimes, but my sis has a heart of gold. You know Sal."

"Yup," said Gilly. "I know Aunt Sal and she's a gem!"

"Have a good week, Tiger!" he said. He gave her a hug and a peck on the cheek. "We will see you in a week and a half! It seems like a long time, but it will go fast. Don't do anything I wouldn't do," he added with a wink.

"Oh, I won't, Dad," she said, winking back.

He closed the door to her room, then stopped, thought a minute, and looked back through the slightly cracked door. Gilly was scribbling notes and calculating in her journal. Her dad shook his head and gently pulled the door closed.

CHAPTER 16

RACE MORNING

Because Alaska is very far north, in the winter months, most of the day is in darkness. In March there may only be daylight from 9:00 am to 3:00 pm. The Iditarod Race started at 9:00 am. Gilly planned to be up by 6:00 am. Dress. Eat. Feed the cats. Rig the sled. Harness up her beasts of the northern wild and head up Main Street by 8:00 am to be well on time for the start. The Wells family lived about ten blocks, just less than a mile, from the starting line downtown. Gilly thought it would be a perfect warmup for the team.

Gilly's parents left at 4:30 am as planned. A taxi picked them up and took them to the Anchorage airport without incident. Unfortunately, at 5:47 am, a raccoon chewed into a transformer two blocks from the Wells house, cutting off all the electricity to the neighborhood. When Gilly had set her plug-in electric alarm that night to wake up at six o'clock, she little expected that there would be a power blackout. The result was that she did not wake up until 8:59 am, less than a minute before the start of the race.

All was lost! She yelped like a cat that'd just had its tail stepped on. Time was everything. Two minutes to microwave her oatmeal. Frantically, she threw on her clothes. She grabbed her already packed backpack (stuffed with an extra hat and socks, her dad's big furry mittens, a space blanket, and other emergency gear) and ran to the barn.

She threw open the barn door like Moses parting the Red Sea. "We are late. We're late. Oh my gosh. I overslept. I'm sorry. We have to hurry!"

Max looked up with a wise and bemused smile. "I'll admit this is not the most propitious start, dear Gilly, but it will all sort out in the end."

"Argh!" shouted Gilly. "We have to hurry!"

Gar walked up and rubbed his whiskers against Gilly's leg. "*Tranquillo!* It is a saying in my country. Relax, sweet cakes. It is a long race and we are not really so very late. What is an hour in a lifetime, eh?"

Gilly was beside herself.

Then Lola said, "Let's just do positive things. Bird by bird. One thing at a time. Life will take care of itself."

"There is always enough time, if one will use it well!" added Max. He had been a well-kept house cat spending many hours at the feet of a retired English professor who read Goethe aloud and talked to him as if he were a student or colleague. Max likely could have passed the SAT college entrance exams.

Still the cats looked on curiously. Most were stretching and yawning. What was the rush? They would get there when they got there! As you know, cats don't wear watches. They are very much of the attitude that things will happen when they happen . . . and not one second sooner.

Gilly was exasperated by their lack of urgency. It took almost forty minutes to get everybody fed, the sled loaded, and the cats harnessed into the towline. Gilly and her cat team left the barn at just after 9:44 am while the dog mushers were streaming out of town toward Willow. At ten thirty, they came trundling down a paw-marked but nearly empty street and ran across the starting line with all the other entries long gone.

Several onlookers later remarked about the rather unbelievable spectacle of a young woman mushing down Main Street with a harness of eight cats long after the dog teams had departed town. She was reportedly wearing a bib that was a striking imitation of a real Iditarod bib, #99. Even more curious was the fact that they actually seemed intent on racing and disappeared down the well-trampled Iditarod trail.

CHAPTER 17

ON THE TRAIL

That first day seemed to last forever. Even though Gilly had cross-country skied more than twenty miles many times, she and the cats picked their way slowly over the rutted trail. Large chunks of snow and ice had been thrown up by the sleds of the mushers who preceded them, which for Gilly and the cats often seemed like snowbanks and icebergs. The trail was scenic and wound through the city greenbelts and paths. Gilly could see people stare at her team of cats as they trundled along. Lights were coming on as darkness fell in mid-afternoon. Finally the trail came up a hill to the culvert under the Campbell Airstrip Road. It was after four in the afternoon. It had taken them almost six hours to go eleven miles.

Banners and evidence of the race hoopla were all about the airstrip, but the mushers and officials were gone. Gilly had not read the fine print in the race announcement. The officials had made a change from the original route due to housing expansion, increased traffic, and congestion on the roads and bridge that crossed the Knik inlet and Matanuska River. Now there was a restart of the race the next day in the town of Willow, some eighty-two miles to the north of Anchorage. The dog mushers had all finished hours ago, had been transported north, and were already setting up in Willow for the restart Sunday morning. Gilly looked about dejectedly. Somehow they had to get to Willow.

CHAPTER 18

THE FIRST NIGHT

Night was falling fast. The darkness was closing in and the temperatures were dropping. "Vell, Boss," said Ravi, "vat now?"

"Well, we can't do much tonight in the dark. I think we had better just camp here for the night right under this big spruce tree. I'll put down my tarp and we can melt snow for water with the cook stove. I've got the tent and we can all huddle up to stay warm. We can figure things out in the morning."

"How do you feel, kid? You okay?" asked Gar. "Hey, we're outdoor cats. We're used to scratching out a living and being cold. We're not those sissified indoor cats you read about in the lower forty-eight who lounge about on the sofa all day batting a catnip-filled mouse. Heck, most of us are downright feral . . . and I say that in the most complimentary way." He had a singsong way of chatting that gave his words a musical quality.

Gilly looked about her at the devoted, scruffy cast of characters. They were all a bit bedraggled, but their spirits were good. "Well," she said with as much cheer as she could muster, "we may be in last place, and a bit off pace, but at least we made the start. We are in the Iditarod! Somehow we will get to Willow," she said firmly.

Under his breath, Shadow muttered, "Yeah, but at this rate,

it will take us a hundred days, past the spring melt, to do the race. Three months to do the whole thing!"

"Hush," said Lola. "Don't worry. Humor the girl. She'll realize that soon enough. We'll turn around in a few days and be back at the barn chasing mice in the haymow. Let her dream."

"Okay, okay. But my feet are cold and I'm getting hungry. Let's go see if we can catch a few mice or voles."

"Hey," said Gilly, "I brought a bag of kibble but we will need to ration our food supplies. It's not great, but it will keep the wolf from the door, as Mom always says."

"Don't say that word," said Max.

"What word?"

"'Wolf,'" said Max. "I'm a tough cat. We are all tough cats. But we ain't 'canis lupus.' We could dodge a bull moose. And the brown bears are hibernating, fortunately. But a wolf pack would make short work of us, I fear."

"They have never had a wolf pack attack a team of huskies in the Iditarod," said Gilly.

"Kid," said Gar, with a raised eyebrow, "we ain't a team of huskies. We're a bevy of felines. We may be tougher pound for pound, but even Max ain't gonna whup a wolf no matter what!"

"The easy out for us would be to climb a tree," said Jami.

"But ve couldn't leave you on da ground, Gilly," said Sasha. "Ve sink or swim together."

"Let's just hope and pray we avoid those denizens of the deep dark forest," muttered Max.

The moon was rising through the trees. It was waxing and nearly full. A great snowy owl, the boreal guardian, flew overhead, eying the little band of travelers tucked beneath the protective overhang of the pine tree. It hooted, its yellow eyes glinting in the night. He sat on the top of a tall white pine through the night and watched the travelers with growing interest.

One by one, Gilly and the cats crawled inside the tent. Overcome by tiredness, they slept peacefully in the still winter air, snuggled together for warmth around the young musher in her sleeping bag.

CHAPTER 19

A LUCKY RIDE TO WILLOW

They broke camp in the morning at about 7:00 am. Gilly had meticulously chosen her survival gear, but it took longer than expected to get it all packed back in the sled. Her supplies included: a bivy sack, a down parka, her long jacket with the fur ruff, her sleeping bag, a whisper-light stove, a small cook pot, a bag of rice, twenty packs of dehydrated food, a bag of trail mix, the large bag of kibble, a large cat bowl, a water jug, a lightweight tent, a folding saw, her map, her GPS, a compass, a flashlight, sunglasses, blizzard goggles, a repair kit, a collapsible shovel, an emergency kit including matches and fire-starter, her headlamp, an axe, a pair of snowshoes, two extra pairs of socks, fully insulated mitts, an extra down jacket, a spare hat and face mask, and her journal.

They walked back up to the parking lot alongside the airstrip. As they were standing there, an old gentleman in a dented, powder-blue F-100 pickup truck pulled up beside them. "Lost?" he asked kindly.

"Not really," Gilly replied. "But we need to get to Willow for the restart of the Iditarod tomorrow."

"Hmpf," said the old gentleman. He had a big, bristly mustache and was sipping a cup of coffee. "Somebody you know in the big race?"

"Yes," said Gilly. "We missed our ride. We need to rendezvous before noon, but the sooner the better."

"Well, I'm going through there on my way to Talkeetna to visit my daughter. I kin give you a lift, I guess. Let's load yer sled in the back. Are the cats ok sitting in the open-air truck bed?"

"I think so," she replied. The cats tilted their heads, as cats will do, and looked back at her quizzically, as if they didn't understand a word of the conversation.

Then, in cat speak, Gar mewed to Gilly, "If it saves tread wear on my tender little feets, then it's just fine with me."

The gentleman put his hand out. "My name is Walter Green, but everybody calls me Bud. Enjoying my retirement, but need things to do. Lost my wife two years ago."

"I'm sorry," said Gilly.

"So I drive around on the weekends and pick up trash. Clean up the environment. Do my bit, you know."

"That's nice," said Gilly. "My mom's a veterinarian and my dad's a newspaper editor."

"You're not the Wells kid by any chance?"

"Yup. My name is Gillian. Most people call me Gilly."

"You were just a peanut last time I saw you. Yer growing up! Pleased to meet you, Miss Gilly. You need to call anybody to let 'em know where yer at?"

"Not right now. We aren't expected for a while," Gilly replied.

"Well, let's get moving. The day is a wasting as my pappy used t' say."

The drive took almost two hours. Finally they pulled into Willow. "Now, you have a way to get home, don't you?" Bud asked Gilly.

"Sure," she said. Under her breath she whispered, "But it's Nome first, then home." As he was driving away, she waved and hollered, "Thanks, Mr. Green!"

"Bud," he corrected her.

"Right!" said Gilly.

CHAPTER 20

A SIGN OF THINGS TO COME

It was almost 10:00 am. The rest of the mushers had already departed earlier in the morning. Gilly and her team again were looking at flapping Iditarod banners and deserted streets. Most of the crowd had seen the real mushers racing off into the wilderness and had already gone home. Gilly hitched the cats to the sled and they set off towards the restart line.

As they approached, a big tan-and-black mongrel came running at them, barking and growling. He snarled and snapped viciously at the cat team from a few feet away. The felines, as one, arched their backs, their hair standing up in crest-like spikes. They snarled back. The husky got a little closer, and Max, with his long reach, cuffed the dog on the nose. His long, untrimmed claws left deep gashes in the dog's muzzle, and the hound ran yelping down the street.

"Nice work," said Shadow.

"Think nothing of it," said Max.

"Ok," said Gilly, "enough distractions. Let's really start this race! Into the wild. Let's go! Hiya! Hiya!" she cried.

And they were off. Eight cats and one young lady with a preposterous belief that they could travel nearly a thousand miles, 998 to be exact, across the Alaskan wilderness. It was perhaps one of the most cockamamie, misconceived, but bold and courageous things ever attempted. There were a few people still at the restart who later commented on the cheeky young lady and her team of cats who raced off into the woods long after the official mass of nearly seventy dog teams had departed.

"Must be a publicity stunt or a commercial for a cat food company, eh, Norton?" speculated a beefy fellow leaning against his truck. The man was sipping a steaming cup of mocha moose coffee.

"But where's the cameras?" his partner muttered. "I doan git it." He took another bite of his glazed donut and belched.

And with that, bib #99 faded into the distance.

CHAPTER 21

CROSSING THE SUSITNA RIVER

Because of the delay getting to Willow, early afternoon found the intrepid adventurers only eight miles down the trail. They were actually making much better time than the day before, though clearly were still far behind. But it wasn't the cats' fault. They were pulling devotedly and their attitude was stellar. The bigger sleds had left a deep track that was wider than Gilly's sled, and so they had to break their own trail. Their sled, fully loaded, was heavier than expected and sank into the snow. In spots, the track was glazed and icy. But off the trail it was worse, with three feet of snow on either side that could swallow Gilly, the cats, and the sled so completely that they wouldn't be found till the spring melt.

At about 2:00 pm they approached the crossing of the Susitna River. The trail had run over a makeshift bridge that had been constructed out of a large fallen tree and additional timbers to widen the path. Sheets of plywood were then covered with snow by a four-wheel ATV to allow the mushers to cross without danger. Unfortunately, the swollen river had washed out part of the crossing during the late morning after all the other mushers had crossed. There was a thirty-foot segment of trail missing! How could they get across?

Gilly and the cats sat looking at the raging waters, crestfallen and disheartened. None of them could survive the freezing, turbulent waters. To attempt to wade the river would result in hypothermia or death by freezing. And most cats, as you know, are notoriously averse to water, not to mention cold water! The river ran north and south, but where they might find a crossing they did not know. It could take days to find an alternate route. All seemed lost.

Upriver, Gilly heard a chittering sound. Then a loud slap resonated in the cold air. She looked about curiously, but could see nothing. Then a voice said, "Why so glum?"

Gilly looked all around but could see no one.

There was a cough, "Ahem," and the voice said, "Down here!"

Gilly looked down the embankment to the water's edge. There she saw a furry face and two bright eyes in the water. It was a beaver.

"Who are you?" she asked.

"Name's Castor. Cass for short. Seems like you need to cross the river, eh? I saw a whole passel of dogsled teams go by before the bridge collapsed late in the morning. Tough luck!"

"We have to get across!" said Gilly.

"What's the hurry?"

"We're in the Iditarod! That's why!"

"You? With cats instead of dogs? Now I've seen everything."

"Can you help us?" implored Gilly.

"Why should I?" asked Cass.

"Well," said the girl, "I'm not a trapper, and the cats have probably been nicer to beavers than dogs have, historically speaking."

Castor laughed. "Yer probably right about that." His eyes twinkling, Castor asked the cats, "So you guys don't want to just swim over?"

All eight felines looked at Cass like he was crazy. They offered a collective scowl. Then Lola said most diplomatically, "Mr.

Beaver, Cass, if there is any way you could help us, help Gilly, to cross over the river, we would be in your debt."

"Let's see what we can do," said Cass. He turned upriver and whistled sharply. Three heads popped up in the water behind him. "We gotta damn up the river, boys!" He spoke with conviction. "Let's go!"

Barely an hour later, they had chewed down and felled a small copse of birch trees that now lay wedged and tangled across the river. The beavers had further packed smaller branches into the crosshatching of trunks and large branches.

Gilly unharnessed all the cats so that none might be caught on branches or pulled into the water if another fell. Gilly pulled the sled across herself, and made two separate trips for the sled's precious cargo. They all crossed safely.

Gilly turned to Cass. "You are a true and unexpected friend! Thank you from the bottom of my heart!"

"Think nothing of it," said Cass. "Damming rivers is what we do. There were rumors of your coming. Good luck and travel safely!" Before Gilly could ask "What rumors?" he slapped his tail on the surface, dove beneath the water, and was gone.

"How lucky can you get?" said Gilly to the cats.

"Actually," said Lola, "it almost seems that someone may be watching over us!"

"No time to dally," added Shadow. "Let's go!"

High above in the thick pine tops, the magnificent white snowy owl looked down on the intrepid travelers. His eyes were dark embers and his beak scythe-like. He had long yellow talons that firmly grasped the branch on which he watched the little crew enter the darkness.

CHAPTER 22

WOLVERINE

A few hours later, in the darkening gloom, they pulled off the trail in a sheltered clearing. Gilly pitched the camp beneath a large fir with an overhang free of snow. She was well aware of the Jack London story "To Build a Fire." By the time they got the tent up and all were fed and watered, the moon was well into the night sky. Everyone was a bit on edge and restless.

Gilly finally fell asleep curled in the midst of her cats. She slept fitfully and had troubled dreams. She was running through deep snow being chased in darkness by a moose, then a brown bear, and finally a howling pack of wolves. Her sled and her cats were running away from her, abandoning her; they were far in the distance. She couldn't catch them and was left alone in the dark forest with her pursuers closing in. She shouted and yelled and then fell into the smothering snow.

Suddenly a fierce snarling erupted outside the tent. Gilly was instantly awake, unsure whether to be more horrified by her dream or the frightening growls outside. In the moonlight, she saw an ominous confrontation. Max, Ravi, and Sasha stood face-to-face with a savage wolverine that weighed nearly as much as the three of them put together. Its teeth snapped wickedly in the cold night air. A wolverine was a buzz saw with attitude, and pound for pound there wasn't anything meaner in the forest. The other five cats had circled Gilly like a family of musk ox to protect their young.

The wolverine snarled, "Give her to me, kitties! I'm quite hungry, and she looks like a juicy young morsel. I've never had much liking for cat meat, but human is another matter. I've picked a few carcasses clean, old miners and the errant hiker or climber who went missing in the woods and died on the trail. Always wanted to savor some fresh, succulent, two-legged young'un. So back off and let me have her. It won't be pretty if I have to take her from you."

"Back off, Jack!" hissed Sasha.

"Don't be inhospitable, pretty lady," said the wolverine in a greasy voice. "Besides, my name ain't Jack, it's Hugh. But that's neither here nor there. You got what I want. And I aim to get it, whether there's one or nine of you kit-kats. I am more than a match for all of ya. Yer out of your domain here. This is my forest. Now git!"

"Leave us in peace!" said Max grimly.

Hugh's body was rumbling and quivering and his eyes glowed red. He snarled and then, without warning, charged toward the girl.

At the moment of his forward leap, a gray blur erupted from the nearby snowbank, and a whirlwind of flashing claws and teeth landed on the back of the wolverine. There was yowling and howling, screaming and tearing, snarling and gnarling, until the wolverine growled, "What the devil? Who challenges me? This is my prey. I found it, and by the law of the forest I claim it as my own."

A large tawny mottled lynx, a ghost of the northern forest, had materialized from nowhere and leapt upon the startled wolverine. Bullies are especially sensitive to being beaten at their own game of surprise and intimidation. Hugh was no exception.

"And by the law of the forest that recognizes my feline clan,

I trump your claim!" The lynx was nearly equal in weight to the wolverine but far better equipped with her large padded feet to fight in deep snow. With the advantage of surprise, she had bested Hugh.

Hugh sat back, dazed and bloodied. The odds were clearly no longer in his favor. He looked savagely at the newcomer. "I know you. Simone ze Lynx. You can float on the snow now, but wait until summer when I have good purchase under my feet. You'll sing a different tune. You have ruined my hunt. I will not forget it." He glowered with an ugly, menacing snarl and backed away from the pack of nine felines. One hundred pounds of feisty cats and a hot-blooded lynx were more than the wolverine could handle. "We will meet again."

Simone sat back, looked at Hugh with a cool savoir faire demeanor, raised her eyebrow, and said, "Do as you will, my rank, musty friend. Trust me, I take your threats seriously. But these are my people, my kin, and the girl is with them. So you lose, Hugh. You will not be dining with them or on them tonight, eh? Go chase some lemmings or chew on an old deer carcass. Au revoir!"

The wolverine lurched through the snow and retreated into the darkness. They could hear him snarling and growling as he crashed through the alder thickets in his furious retreat. Under his breath, he muttered, "You don't mess with Hugh the Wolverine. Maybe a word to some four-legged lupine friends will cure you of your haughty feline attitudes. Woe to whomever crosses my path."

They stood in a little circle outside the tent. "Thank you, Simone, for saving us, saving me, from the wolverine," said Gilly.

"It was nothing," said the Canadian lynx. "He is a rascal at best and a scoundrel at worst. An opportunist with a mean streak a mile long. He gives my forest a bad name. I apologize for his bad behavior. But to the task at hand. You are trying to run to Nome. I admire your verve, as we would say in Quebec. I am French Canadian originally, you see. I feel obligated and privileged, as a fellow cat, to help you, if you will accept my assistance. I know ze way, and I should give you some extra muscle in the traces, oui?"

"Oh, Simone," said Gilly, "this is fantastic! Now we are nine cats pulling in the harness. Everything is now as it was supposed to be! What do you say, team?"

With a resounding "Meow!" Simone was welcomed to the team.

"Get some sleep now," purred Simone. "I will watch outside tonight."

CHAPTER 23

THE NINTH CAT

Gilly awoke the next morning to the screaming of a robber jay. There was frost on her eyelashes and inside of the tent. Each breath produced plumes of vapor. She was cold.

The night before seemed like a dream. Had a wild lynx named Simone really rescued them from a vicious wolverine? As she wiggled in the sleeping bag, she heard a yowl and a hiss.

"Hey, watch it, Gilly. That's my tail." It was Gar, muttering, as the cats began stirring, one by one, and opened sleepy eyes.

Outside a voice snarled, "Sacre bleu! Get up, you sleepyheads. We have a race to run!" Simone stood impatiently outside the tent, her large furry feet floating on the snow where the feet of others punched through.

They scrambled from the tent and stood obediently before the elegant north woods lynx.

Che and Gar were very impressed by the elegant and jaunty Simone. The cats all admired her ferocity and knowledge of the woods. She gave them some credibility—"street cred" or "woods cred." Lola was secretly jealous of Simone's lineage but was glad she was on their side.

Gilly spent a half hour splicing a larger collar onto the harness and tug line to allow Simone to assume the lead position. The squabbling and doubts of yesterday had given way to a new optimism. Suddenly, their chances didn't seem so meager, nor the race so long. The risks that had worried them before in the light of day seemed like hobgoblins of the night, and faded away.

Gilly poured kibble out onto the tent floor for her companions. They devoured it. Then, Gilly melted snow and poured the water into the bowl she carried in the sled. They lapped it up. Simone beckoned them outside. She had caught some mice and a rabbit that she shared with the team. Well fed, they were now ready to run.

Gilly dropped the tent. She shook the snow off the fly, folded it, and stowed it on the sled. With Simone now in the lead, they set off at a brisk pace. Things were looking up! Life was good. Simone brought a new joie de vivre to the team. The sun was bright. The trail lay clear before them, trampled by the dogs and sleds that had long preceded them.

"We may be last, but at least it's easy going," said Shadow to Lola.

"Yes," said Ravi, "and I do not vish to tangle with any of those huskies. Big attitude problem, you know vat I mean?"

"Look, ve'll go till the kid gets tuckered out and then head for home. A little bit cold and sore, some excitement, no harm done, eh?" said Sasha. "Besides, ve owe Gilly for rescuing us, don't ve?"

"Ja, mon!" said Gar.

CHAPTER 24

MOOSE ATTACK

They ran at an easy loping pace, the nine cats drawing the sled along smoothly. Simone allowed them to increase their speed and mileage by almost half again as much. She proved to be a keen judge of the trail and always seemed to pick the best route when the track got ragged. Gilly jogged along behind, holding tightly to the sled. Occasionally she would rest a foot on the back runner as all mushers do when the trail was smooth or had a downhill slope. The cats pulled strongly and seemed to have developed a natural rhythm and synergy that made the morning fly by. Gilly calculated that they had covered almost fifteen miles by early afternoon. Things seemed to be picking up!

Suddenly, there was a crashing sound in the bushes ahead and a giant shape loomed over them.

"Meow! Yeow! Holy cow!" screeched Lola. An enormous bull moose with a huge rack of antlers blocked the path. It snorted wildly and pawed the trail into a mishmash, digging up dirt, pine needles, and old composting leaves. Spittle flew in all directions from its blubbering lips. Tendrils of mucous and goobers of snot dangled and swung from its flaring nostrils.

The cats all had the same thought at once: "Climb a tree! Get above this crazy ruminant before we all get trampled!" But they all simultaneously realized that they couldn't climb a tree harnessed together to the sled. And more importantly, they couldn't abandon Gilly to this berserk snorting beast. So they stood their ground, and stared with steely eyes at the clearly irrational and monstrous creature. They all knew that moose were the most dangerous threat to any sled dog or musher on the trail. What hope did they have against this thousand-pound behemoth?

Finally Max shouted, "Hey, Moose! What gives? We got no bone to pick with you. We are just out for a quiet run with the kid through the forest. Let us by and we will get out of your hair! We mean no harm."

The moose, who didn't have very good eyesight, squinted at them. He took a step forward and almost stepped on Simone.

"Sacre bleu, Mssr. Moose! Watch that dinner plate–sized hoof!" shouted Simone. As an aside to Jami, "We do not travel in ze same social circles, you know."

Gilly raised a mittened hand in greeting. "Hi Moose," she said.

"Humph," said the moose at last, looking them up and down. "Why, you are just cats and a little girl. But with a lynx in the mix? Hmmm. Curiouser and curiouser. What are you doing out here, in my forest, in the middle of winter?"

"We are racing in the Iditarod," said Gilly. "See, we even have an entry bib." Gilly held up bib #99.

"Heavens ta Murgatroid! Now I have seen everything. I thought you were another one of those sled dog teams trespassing and fouling my domain. Dog poop is a mess! You ever step in that caca? Yech!"

"We are very tidy and neat. You know how cats are. Spotless!" said Lola.

"I gotta admit, you guys were so darn quiet, you startled the heck out of me. The doggies are a raucous lot and remind me too much of their cousin wolfies, who are my archenemies. I am

willing to give you the benefit of the doubt. Besides, I heard you were coming and was told to help you if you needed it. Are you sure you know what you're doing?"

All the cats looked at Gilly and Gilly looked at her team. "Who told you we were coming?"

"Not for me to say, but you can never have too many allies," said the seven-foot-tall monster. "I will call ahead and see if some of my brethren down the trail can slow your competitors down a bit." He gave them a sly grin and a myopic wink. "And be careful along the next riverbank; it's running high. Stay on the right of the trail by the fallen pine. So scoot along, and good luck!"

He turned and walked back towards the woods, shaking his antlers. Then he stopped, looked around, and said, "I heard some howling last night that wasn't from huskies. Go quietly and keep your ears on!" And he disappeared into the dark thicket of conifers.

The cats looked at one another with some concern. "Whatcha think, Gilly? If we turn around, we'd be home tomorrow in a warm bed." It wasn't clear who spoke.

"We can do this!" said Gilly. "We are going fast now. We have the moose as a friend. I know we can make it."

"It is a long, long journey, Gilly child. Grown men and big dogs fail and are broken on this trail," said Shadow solemnly.

Gilly looked crestfallen, sensing the confidence of her team failing around her. There were tears in her eyes. "Is this the way you all feel?"

The cats looked at each other and kneaded the snow with their paws.

"Look," said Max, "let's give it another day, but then maybe we should think about turning back, huh? We compromise! We want you safely at home when your parents get back, okay?"

High above, the snowy owl followed their progress. He too

had heard the howling in the distance. His wings lifted him into the night sky and he went to see what the noise was all about.

With Simone in the lead-cat position, they covered over forty miles that day. They passed Yentna and were partway to Skwentna. At about 9:00 pm they stopped for the evening to rest. Gilly was developing a routine of pitching camp, building a fire, feeding the cats, and melting water. She was well aware that in 1985 a moose had killed two of Susan Butcher's dogs and injured others so that she had to drop out of the race. Gilly was lucky and she knew it. They sat around the fire reviewing the day, chatting and "catting" to get to know Simone better. Despite their highly attuned senses, they still did not know they were being watched.

CHAPTER 25

UKPIK

The snowy owl hooted and rose from the branch like a white angel against the blackness of the night sky. He whirled into the air and disappeared between the dense trees. There was a fading flutter of wings and the rustle of the wind. Gilly and the cats heard a soft "Whoooooooooo" and, again, "whoooarrrrrreeyooooouuu," and then there was silence. They were all looking up to where the snowy owl had last faded into the sky.

Then a branch snapped on the ground just beyond the firelight. All eyes were now focused to the ground and the dark periphery beyond the tree trunks. Nothing moved. No one breathed. Was it the bull moose? A bear? The wolves? Horrific visions filled Gilly's mind. Then there was a flicker of movement in the shadows between the corrugated pine trunks. The outline of a large form became visible. The cats circled around Gilly protectively. Instinctively, she grasped the crocodile's tooth on its worn leather lanyard that her father had given her for protection. It seemed to be rattling between her fingers.

There was a sudden movement. A scratching sound. A red glint of light, like a ruby, flared in the darkness, a single blood-red eye: a match. Held in a gnarled, brown hand. Two black, creased eyes shone behind the glow of the light. A pipe was being lit. The figure of a man materialized and walked slowly toward them.

He was a big man wrapped in a fur robe. He had long dark hair and a sharp aquiline nose. There were scars on his cheeks. His brow was furrowed. A bead necklace hung about his neck. A small leather pouch hung beneath the necklace.

"What do you want?" Gilly declared. "Who are you?"

"Who am I?" came the reply in a voice soft like the wind. "Who are you?"

"I'm Gilly Wells. And these are my friends, my sled team. Lola, Shadow, Max, Sasha, Ravi, Gar, Che, Jamila, and Simone." Each nodded gracefully, but kept his or her eyes fixed on the stranger.

"Ah yes! I have heard of you." He placed his finger against his nose and looked up from his glowing pipe, issuing a thin spiral of smoke into the cool air. They could see that his eyes, although creased with years, were kind and wise. And he smiled, not as an amused adult, but as one views a respected opponent or an admired adversary, a worthy ally or friend.

"All the forest is abuzz with your coming," said the old man.

"They are? All the forest?"

"They are, from moose to wolverine to owl to robber jay, to raven, eagle, pine marten, snowshoe hare, to caribou, to sheep, and, it seems, to wolf. Only the hibernating brown bear is insensible to your presence in their woods. It is good that the bear, *ursus horribilis*, is sleeping, as he, or especially she, can sometimes be very cross, very irritable indeed, to the presence of unannounced or unwelcome visitors. Some would say you trespass, but then, you are hardly the yowling noisy claptrap of the sled dog teams that have preceded you. And lead you by a sizeable distance, I might add. Yes, all the denizens of the forest have heard of the young pale girl and her brave, or perhaps foolhardy, feline companions who are chasing the Iditarod mushers into the Alaskan wild."

Gilly was silent.

"The question," said the man, "is *why*?"

"*Why*?" stammered Gilly.

"Yes. *Why* do you, a small, young girl creature, who presumably has a warm bed in a home somewhere safe with loving parents, enter a dark and frozen wasteland in a race that has defeated many, broken others, and killed some. It is not a meager thing. And with cats of all things!"

"Well," she finally sputtered with some indignation, "because I've always wanted to run the Iditarod. It's been my dream. And this was my chance. Our chance. It is our adventure!"

There was a pause, and then the man said, "That is all the reason you need, my young adventurer. 'Because!' is good enough. I admire that gumption. You have a pure heart and faithful, brave companions. But you need more than innocence and courage."

"What more?" Gilly asked.

"Yeah, what more?" murmured the cats.

"You need strength, a protector, or both. It is a basic fact of life."

"I guess it's too late for that now, eh?" murmured Gilly.

"Oh no. In fact, this is the perfect time, the purrfect time! You have committed to this adventure. And here I am."

"And who are you?" asked Ravi.

"I have many names, but among my Athabaskan people I am known as Ukpik. Some would call me a shaman. I was gifted to be a shape-shifter and a soul mender. The snowy owl, Boreas, is my talisman and my bird form. My people were always here. We have been here as long as the bear and moose. We were born of the river, the hills, and the sun. There was no time when we were not here, not a part of this place. Every molecule of my body was at one time part of the sea brine, the air, and the tundra."

"You are a shape-shifter?" Gilly had heard of the sacred wise men and women who could assume the form of any creature and had powers to heal.

"Yes, small one, I am. All life is transformation. We transition from one life to another over and over again. We are born to breathe this air and later become the earth. We float in the ocean and are consumed by fire. We become a leaf and are eaten by a caterpillar that becomes a butterfly that is eaten by a bird that becomes food for the pine marten that is food for the wolf, and so on. The wolf and the moose and the bear are food for the earth, for worms and flowers and trees, and it all comes round again and again and again. It is the endless rapture of life."

Ukpik sat on a bough of pine needles smoking his pipe, appraising them.

"You need a protector for the days ahead." He reached around his neck and removed the small leather pouch. He held it forward to the girl. "Wear this, Gilly." He pronounced her name "je-lay" as if she were an exotic and holy thing.

She stepped forward and took the leather pouch from his gnarled hands. She dropped the necklace over her head. The pouch was soft, as if filled with a powder or ash. She felt an electric buzz run through her, and the earth seemed to sway beneath her feet. "What is this?"

"It is a sacred amulet. It is my blessing of protection for you and those who protect you. In short, it is a magic talisman that will help you in time of danger or need."

"How will it help me . . . us?"

"I cannot say. That depends on the danger you face and the courage you need. Do not call upon its power unless your predicament is dire."

"But . . ."

"I must go," Ukpik said, rising from the ground. He was lithe and agile in his movements, despite his years. He removed the pipe from his mouth. "You are a brave young woman. And you have brave comrades. Your vision and dream is very strong."

He laid his palm on each cat in turn; each felt the passing of a greater presence. "Guard her well," he said to them.

Then he turned and began chanting in a soft rumbling voice, like an Australian didgeridoo, if you have ever heard one, a throaty, vibrating incantation. He began turning round and round, faster and faster, until his fur robe swirled out to the sides. The snow whirled about him in a flurry. A cone-like vortex of swirling snow enveloped his body in whiteness and rose upwards above his head. He disappeared in the miasma.

From the top of the gyration of snow emerged the great snowy owl, regal and beautiful. Boreas flapped into the night air and was gone without a sound.

CHAPTER 26

THE NIGHT OF THE WOLVES

In the morning, the bundle of cats wrapped around the girl began to stir with the first light. There were purrs, eyes blinking and paws stretching, but this morning, no one really seemed inclined to move.

Gilly was still in her sleeping bag. She reached for the leather amulet about her neck. It was still there. So it hadn't been a dream. Ukpik was real. They had a protector. An Athabaskan shaman who was watching over them in the form of a snowy owl! "Holy cow," she muttered.

Simone stuck her head inside the tent, for she had slept outside, as was her lifelong habit. "It es a very good thing, this shaman, Ukpik. Now we pick up ze pace, eh?"

The rest of the cats nodded in agreement.

After a few yawns, Jamila stood on all four limbs, arched her back a few times in classic cat pose, and exhaled. Her breath left a vapor trail that hung in the air.

"Could be colder somewhere, I suppose," she muttered. "Like maybe Antarctica."

"Ha," laughed Gilly. "Dad and I camped out in forty below zero once. Piece of cake."

"Fahrenheit or celsius?"

"They're the same at forty below!"

"If this hairless Mowgli child can endure the cold, certainly we can too!" muttered Che. "Why do you think God gave you fur?"

"I'll admit it's a little nippy. But we'll warm up once we start moving. Ain't that right, Gar?"

"Ya mon! We've got some miles to keep today."

Simone smiled at the cat chatter. "This is balmy weather, my tropical friends. Let's take advantage of it!"

They were soon back on the trail, which was well trampled by the dogs and sleds that had gone before. No new snow had fallen, so the trail was easy to follow. It stretched before them like the yellow brick road to Oz, colored by stained stretches of yellow dog pee and covered with turds.

"It's a fact of nature," said Max. "Gotta keep hydrated. Keeps the juices jangling. Satchel Paige, the great pitcher, said that!"

"He also said, 'Don't look back . . . something might be gaining on you,'" said Shadow uneasily.

At the end of that fourth day, they pulled off the trail into a clearing to rest for the night. It had been a long day, the hardest day of the race so far. But they had run through Skwentna and Finger Lake for a total of fifty-two miles. It was their greatest distance in a day yet. But even at this speed, they would be on the trail for over three weeks. They had covered 127 miles in four days and had 871 miles to go.

The cats were exhausted. Gilly was exhausted. She mechanically set up the tent and fired the stove to melt snow for water. She built a fire for light and safety. She fed the cats with the dwindling supply of food. Then she collapsed into her tent and curled up in her sleeping bag. She always left her tent door open so that the cats could come and go. They often slept inside with her for warmth, but might step outside during the night if nature called or the moon captured their fancy.

This was a dark night. The stars were faint. The moon, though starting to wane, was obscured by clouds. The landscape was shadowed. There were no moonbeams this night.

In the distance, a single yip was followed by an echoing howl. It seemed far away, yet not so far. Deep in sleep, Gilly heard the sounds, and though she shuddered, she did not awaken.

Hugh had done his work to sow the seeds of discord among his four-legged lupine friends. Stealthily, the wolf pack approached the sleeping party. They were masters of slipping through the woods unseen and unheard. And their approach towards the young girl and her contingent of feline companions was as silent as the night.

Cats, of course, have extraordinary senses of their own. Simone was suddenly alert, looking at the distant woods with her steely gaze. And when the wind shifted slightly, Che and Gar lifted their heads simultaneously, detecting a change in the night air. Soon all nine cats were on guard, their olfactory senses and sixth sense tingling with the approach of the unseen foe.

"Pssst," said Simone to Gilly. "We have visitors."

Gilly rubbed her eyes and sat up. "What?"

"Wolves," said Shadow in a whisper.

The fire that Gilly had built before going to sleep had now died down to dim coals. It offered barely a glow to the clearing in which they were camped.

Suddenly there was a guttural snarl outside at the edge of the trees encircling the tent. Gilly pushed aside the tent flap and looked into the darkness. The faint glimmer of firelight reflected off the retinas of some ten pairs of wolf eyes. She could not see the sharp teeth that she knew accompanied each grim visage.

Gilly picked up some branches and threw them on the fire. It flared and cast the clearing into a flickering light. Shadows danced against the tall pines. The cats had emerged from the tent behind her.

A lone black she-wolf, Sable, stepped into the clearing. Her eyes were glowing embers and her fangs were ivory daggers.

"What do you want?" asked Gilly softly.

Sable smiled as only a wolf can smile. "I do not answer to you," she said in a measured, sinister voice. "You have chosen to trespass on our hunting grounds, and you bring felines, our lifelong foe, into our sacred forest. I have allowed men to live for being stupid and alone, but when your companions are my sworn enemy, there is little room for mercy. Besides, I understand you have humiliated our friend Hugh, the wolverine. He is a simple fellow, but he is predictable and can be counted on in times of trouble. What do you have to say for yourselves?" asked Sable.

"We come in peace," replied Gilly. "We mean no harm." Remembering Kipling's *Jungle Book*, and Mowgli's successful oaths to the lords of the jungle, she addressed the she-wolf and cried, "'We be of one blood, ye and I!'"

"Oh, we will be soon, young one, very soon. Nice try with the 'Law of the Pack' thing."

"You don't honor the Law of the Pack? What about Akela, leader of the wolves? In Kipling's tale, this is a sacred thing!" said Gilly, now very frightened.

"I wasn't much of a student," said Sable, her tone changing from silky to menacing. "Don't know this Kipling fellow, and I have no need for books. I studied survival. Unfortunately, my dear, you are in the wrong place at the wrong time. And we are hungry, very hungry. Quite literally famished. Not good for you."

She began to slowly step forward, oblivious to the dancing flames of the fire. Behind her, the wolf pack, ten strong, stepped into the light of the clearing. They were gaunt and had wild, crazed eyes. Their ribs showed through their fur. They looked at Gilly and the cats with a rabid intensity.

Gilly was terrified. She took a deep breath and clasped her sheath knife grimly in her hand. The cats prepared for a battle to the death. They knew they had no chance. They all stepped in front of Gilly.

Simone shouted at the black wolf, "Sable! This will not serve your pack well. If you kill a human, you will be hunted mercilessly to the ends of the earth. You know this! Leave the girl alone!"

"Simone, Simone. You disappoint me. Hunger knows no bounds. You have picked the wrong time to side with the two-legs. And your domestic feline companions are hardly a match for us. They are merely appetizers, kibble, one might say, for my pack. Trust me, there won't be a bone of evidence left. You should run and climb up that tree while you can. At least save yourself." She gave her a toothy grin. "Bon appétit, puddy tat!"

The great black wolf leaped into the air toward Gilly and the cats. As she did so, a white projectile plunged from the night sky and struck the wolf full force against the side of its head with raking talons and a powerful beak. It was the snowy owl. The wolf was momentarily stunned, blood dripping from lacerations over its left eye and muzzle.

"What folly is this?" the furious wolf howled. Her pack had closed behind her.

Gilly looked in horror at the raging, bloodied wolf. "Boreas . . . Ukpik!" she cried. Suddenly she remembered the leather pouch around her neck. She reached up and clasped the pouch. It seemed to quiver and jump in her hands. As she tried to pull it from her neck, the pouch burst open so that the powder within flew in a cascading fan over her cats, who stood stalwart before her. It sparkled and glittered in a phosphorescent cloud. The cats seemed crazed by the dust and began running in circles in a widening arc. They were caterwauling and snarling in a crazy fashion. Faster and faster they ran, and the circle began to widen. As the snow swirled about them,

the cats began to blur, and all became a spinning vortex of black, yellow, and gray fur ... until everything stopped.

The wolves, briefly distracted by the owl and the whirlwind, now moved forward to attack. As the whirling dust and maelstrom of snow began to settle, there was a deep, throaty rumble within the cloud of snow and powder. Gilly could see the silhouettes of her faithful cats, but they were somehow changed in a way that she could not at first understand.

When the air cleared, an amazing transformation was revealed. Where once was Ravi now stood a massive Siberian tiger. Sasha, of the Himalayas, had become an elegant snow leopard. Lightning fast, Che had become a cheetah. Jamila had become a spotted leopard. Gar was now a rippling Amazon jaguar. Lola had become a puma, and Shadow a black panther. Max was now a majestic African lion with a golden flowing mane. Even the feral Simone had enlarged twofold into a primordial lynx.

Sasha stepped forward and batted Sable aside like a toy mouse. The black wolf was tossed through the air and lay dazed in the snow. "Are you still hungry, volf? Enough to challenge *my* friends? You do not threaten young girls from now on, you understand? I think you should apologize and leave quickly, before ve too become hungry."

The wolf pack shrunk back in disbelief. Sable, the black wolf, rose to her paws, unsteady, and looked at the great cats. The odor of fear permeated the clearing. She whimpered like a cur. "You are free to travel our forest as you will. Please excuse our intrusion. I beg your forgiveness." And she slunk away, limping, with her tail between her legs, her pack following her into the darkness. Then they turned tail and ran like their lives depended on it, which, in fact, was true. Their howls, forlorn and edgy, echoed through the forest. It was pitiful rather than sinister, as it had been the night before.

Gilly looked about her. "Oh my gosh! she said. "Oh my gosh! What happened?"

"The shaman's dust brought us back to our ancestral form," said Max. "We are still your devoted team, but how long we will remain transformed cannot be said. Often magic is strongest under the cover of night, but we shall see in the morning light if the magic holds. We should run while we can."

"Keep your fingers crossed," said Gilly, with a laugh when she realized what she had said. "Paws crossed!"

As the morning sun broke over their camp on the sixth day, it revealed nine giant felines. Gilly's cats remained enlarged and powerful beyond imagination. The harness traces for the small cats would no longer accommodate her now giant felines. Gilly used her extra rescue rope to fashion new harnesses that she attached at the tug lines to the center towline. She cut strips of her blanket for the necessary harness padding, and with her hand awl, sewed the straps into comfortable collars. Soon all was ready.

As the cats stood waiting, ready to resume the race, Gilly looked up and saw the great snowy owl on a branch above them. "Thank you, *Chin'an*, Ukpik," said Gilly, using the Athabaskan word of gratitude she had learned as a child. "Yes, *Chin'an*, Ukpik," said the great cats as one.

CHAPTER 27

TRANSFORMED

Leaving their camp beyond Finger Lake, Gilly and her team negotiated two hairpin switchbacks on the Happy Canyon trail. They skirted the civilized way stations, as Gilly thought it would be too risky. She didn't know how the humans at the checkpoints would react to her now intimidating team. They passed Rainy Pass, and then descended the twenty-mile stretch into the Dalzell Gorge with its icy precipitous trail. In mid-afternoon they rested for an hour. As the sun sank below the horizon, Gilly again harnessed the great cats to the sled. They passed Rohn and then raced across the desolate ninety-mile stretch called "The Burn." They passed through Nikolai and, near midnight, stopped to camp.

Gilly's cats had traveled thirty-four miles in the first two days, and another ninety-three miles in the two days since Simone had joined the team. It was a great achievement for a young lady and her mostly domestic cats. However, they weren't just out for a stroll in the park; they were in the Iditarod! Most of the leading dog teams averaged more than one hundred miles per day. On that fifth day of their journey, despite a late start, the cats had covered over 170 miles in fifteen hours.

Since the cats' transformation, they could now run 150 to 200 miles a day. Their cruising speed was more than double that of most dog teams. At that pace, they might be able to catch the leaders of the Iditarod in several days . . . if they were lucky. Although their agility, grace, and power were without peer, they had to limit their speed so that they did not whip Gilly and her sled off the trail. As yet, they remained a great distance behind, and the most dangerous segments of the race lay before them. Most of the mushers were already halfway through the journey by now.

The cats rested briefly during the day, drinking snow water that Gilly melted for them and taking catnaps to replenish their strength. During the long hours of darkness, they ran like the wind. When they stopped to rest that evening, the cats went off in pairs to hunt for caribou, deer, or rabbits. It was a necessary business, one they had known and perfected since time began. There would always be hunters and the hunted. It was the way of nature and of all life and existence. At least five or six of the great cats always remained in camp with Gilly for protection.

Their sleep that night was peaceful. Gilly lay alone in her tent. The cats were now far too large to share the space and were more comfortable curled into the snow and against each other to preserve body heat. The girl had no nightmares that night. Her tent was surrounded by the greatest collection of giant felines that had trod the North American continent in 10,000 years. Gilly feared no harm.

CHAPTER 28

THE BLIZZARD

The next day, all the world seemed renewed. Gilly was up early. She was still astounded by the transformation of her cats into these giant felines. They broke camp in darkness well before sunrise and were soon moving swiftly across the windswept Alaskan terrain. They passed through McGrath and Takotna.

In the late morning, the sun cast its northern light on the landscape. Clouds floated across the sky, alternately shielding the sun and opening to allow its rays to warm the earth. They ran through warm patches of sunlight that mottled the snowfield and then into cooler pools of shade. There were dark glens in the forest, illuminated by beams of sunlight that seemed like the hallowed cathedrals of Europe. Ice crystals condensed in the air, floating and shimmering in the light. The squeak of the sled runners on the cold snow and the panting of the great cats were the only sounds to mark their passing. Sometimes they seemed to be traveling alone, the only living beings in a ghost world. Still they ran on.

They passed the skeletons of moose, deer, caribou, dogs, and an old trapper. White bones exposed by the wind stood starkly like porcelain slats beside corrugated tree trunks; others had been dragged by the wolves onto the hard, windswept, and eroded sastrugi snow. There were teeth marks on most of the bones. Wolverines, wolves, pine martens, and rodents had gnawed the bones for calcium or any faint nourishment.

The predatory cycle was relentless and unforgiving. Life went on for some; not for others. One day you may be the hunter and the next you may be food, sustenance, for another. The strong, the cunning, and the relentless most often survived. But nature was an hourglass in which each creature had its day of reckoning. It was a hard lesson, but it was the nature of life. There was no way to soften that truth. For Gilly and the snowcats, it was a good day to keep running. It was their day in the sun.

When they reached Ophir, the trail turned south. Running steadily, they passed through a desolate and barren expanse of windswept tundra on the approach to Iditarod, namesake of the race. Once a bustling gold and mining town, Iditarod was now an abandoned ghost town. The remnant village was part of the Yukon-Koyukuk territory, an area as big as the entire state of Montana but inhabited by fewer than 6,000 people.

In the late afternoon, the wind began to pick up, and soon great flakes of snow began to fall. They had just passed through Iditarod. The swirling snow obscured the waning light of day. It created an eerie glow in the western sky that soon faded into darkness. Gilly pulled her parka up tightly around her face. The fur ruff kept her warm, and she had goggles to protect her eyes. She wore her father's large mitts that were connected to her parka by a secure cord tether so they could not be blown away. The winds continued to blow, scouring the snow from the ground. Then the blizzard began in earnest and the snow drove at them horizontally. The snow came faster and faster. The world closed in. They could see nothing. No outlines, no shadows, not even the hand or paw before the open eye. It was a whiteout and they had to stop.

Gilly circled the cats around the sled. She had noticed a

giant snowdrift near the trail just before losing all sight. Slowly they inched toward the embankment. Once there, Gilly took the snow shovel from her sled and began to dig. Fortunately she was able to scoop into the snowdrift and excavate a large den or snow cave. In a half hour's time, they were all safely inside, protected from the howling wind and raging blizzard. Their body heat caused the snow to glaze on the inside of the cave. Gilly pushed her shovel handle through the top of the cave roof for a ventilation hole. She melted snow for the cats near the opening of the snow shelter.

After they had hydrated and eaten, Gilly lay against Jamila's tawny fur. She started to talk without really thinking. "Don't you marvel at the amazing variety of creatures in the world? The sizes, shapes, colors, wings, tails, teeth, fins, feathers, scales, bills, beaks, claws, and hooves? What a wonder."

"It is a rare and beautiful thing!" said Jami.

"You should come to South America someday," said Gar. "The Amazon jungle is teeming with exotic wildlife: birds such as macaws, quetzals, toucans, flycatchers, and tanagers, sloths, civets, some big snakes, and incredible flowers. It is a kaleidoscope of colors. The birds alone are unbelievable."

"Hmm," countered Jami, "you haven't seen anything until you have seen Africa. Isn't that so, Che?"

"Yes, lady!" he said with a toothy grin. "Giraffes, monkeys, baboons, gorillas, elephants, wildebeests, gnus, ibis, crocodiles, hippos . . . we could go on for hours. It is a cornucopia of critters."

"Ha!" said Ravi. "But in Eurasia, we have pandas, Siberian tigers, snow leopards, - of which Sasha and I are but two examples- our cousins the Amur leopard, the yeti (maybe!), yaks and naks, hawk-like lammergeiers, crocodiles, rhinos, elephants, monal pheasants, and iridescent peacocks. And we have the Himalayas, the most spectacular mountains in the world. Sagarmatha, you know her as Everest, is the mother goddess of peaks and reaches closest to the heavens of any place on earth. Trekking to see her through a rhododendron forest is a miraculous thing. It is a very sacred place."

"I hope to see all your native lands one day!" said Gilly.

And then she paused, realizing the inexplicable wonder of the companions lying around her. "Talk about miracles! Look at you! I mean, how do we explain *you*? Holy cow! It's all too incredible."

The cats looked at one another, not knowing whether to yowl or run. "You are the wonderment, Gilly. That is why we love you," said Lola. Shadow nodded. Gilly blushed.

"Do you want to be a veterinarian like your mom or a writer like your dad?" asked Max.

"I don't know yet," said the girl. "I like science, but I like literature and writing too. I like to compare things. Maybe I will do both!"

"Der is plenty of time to focus as long as you have curiosity. And dat is something ve cats know a bit about, ya, Ravi?" added Sasha. She gave the slumbering Siberian, who was in the middle of a well-deserved catnap, a nudge. Warm in their snow cave, they slept curled together and dreamt good dreams.

CHAPTER 29

THE WENDIGO

The weather cleared the following day and they ran like the wind from early in the morning until late at night, a good sixteen hours. They passed Shageluk, Anvik, Grayling, and Eagle River in succession. The 200-mile stretch between Shageluk and Kaltag was known as an isolated and desolate region. Some described it like "falling off the end of the earth." The winds and the cold were brutal, and the team was often forced to run on the unprotected Yukon River. It was said the wind there could lift your eyelids from your eyeballs. Frozen whirlpools called "suckholes" posed a dangerous threat. Sometimes a thin layer of snow would make these whirlpools nearly invisible except for a faint plume of mist. An entire dog team and musher could plunge into the swirling water and be lost. There was no shelter for the lonely traveler.

Gilly and the cats trusted Simone's careful route choices and negotiated the dangerous Yukon passage without any missteps or accidents. Several times Simone steered them away from areas of open water or snow-covered suckholes that might have ended their journey. The cold bit at them, but they persevered with grit and determination. Gilly was a trooper. They finally stopped for the night in a dark forested area midway between Eagle Island and Kaltag. They had completed 193 miles that day and were now 627 miles into the race. Nome lay 371 miles in the distance, still a long ways away. Gilly figured, with good luck, that they might be able to finish in two days.

They slept hard that evening. Well after midnight, Gilly felt a slight draft of air, and a breeze ruffled the tent flap. She felt the wind curl beneath her sleeping bag as an arm might encircle your waist and pull you forward. It drew her from the tent. Gar and Jamila both watched her curiously as she stepped outside. Simone sat alertly beside the tent, sniffing the air. "I don't like it," she said. "Something feels wrong, but I can't quite figure out what it is."

Gilly had walked only a few paces from the tent. Standing at the edge of the clearing, she looked up at the treetops, as if drawn to something ethereal above.

"Don't wander too far, Gilly!" said Gar.

"Hmmm," sighed Gilly, still half asleep. "Don't you hear it?" she asked them. "Someone needs help. Someone is calling, 'Oh, my feet, my burning feet of fire.'" She took another step and looked up. The wind rushed at them from above, and a swirling shape descended from the treetops toward the girl.

"Mon Dieu," shouted Simone. "Ze Wendigo! Run, Gilly, run!"

But before the girl could move, a brutish creature with black leathery wings, a curving beak, sharp talons and a serpentine tail swooped down and lifted Gilly into the sky. It was a grotesque beast that appeared part hyena, part pterodactyl, and part snake. Its sunken green eyes had a vertical black crescent iris that gleamed with an evil reptilian intent.

Jamila, Gar, and Simone all leaped into the air to try to intercept the creature, but it was too fast, and they all fell back to the ground with empty claws.

"Awake, awake!" cried Simone. "The Wendigo has Gilly!"

The cats were outside in a second. "What do we do?" they snarled. "What is it? What is a Wendigo?"

"It is a demon of the dark northern wilderness and a cruel, evil spirit. We must follow it as quickly as we can, or risk losing her forever! It may not be able to carry her far before . . . Hurry!"

As Simone spoke, Gilly was aloft at the level of the treetops. She was wide awake now and shouted frantically to her cats by name; they tracked her on the ground by her cries. She grasped the amulet about her neck and whispered, "Ukpik, Boreas, help me!" But this time neither the owl nor the shaman appeared to save her, and there was no more magic dust.

The stench of the creature overwhelmed her with an odor of decay and death. Its skin was leathery and coarse with a bristly plumage. Like a hideously magnified housefly, it had stiff, barbed spines and a grotesquely scaled head. The eyes, pushed back into the sockets, glared at her. Gilly was clenched in its cruel, taloned claw, and she gasped to draw a breath. "I can't die," she vowed to herself. "I can't let it kill me." She knew this battle was hers alone.

She reached to her waist and pulled her musher's knife from its sheath. Without a moment's remorse, she plunged the steel blade as deeply as she could into the Wendigo's chest and twisted the blade as hard as she could. The creature screamed with pain and anger. Unfortunately, the blade could not penetrate the massive pectoral wing muscles. The beast writhed and shook so that Gilly lost her grip on the knife, and it fell to the ground eighty feet below.

The Wendigo was now enraged. "You can prick me with your little dagger, my dear, but it won't save you. A few scratches won't stop me." Gilly struck at the creature with her fists with little effect. Then, reaching in her shirt, Gilly grasped the crocodile's tooth that her father had given her. With all the strength she could muster, she jabbed it into the right eye of the foul creature. The Wendigo writhed in pain and uttered a hideous, bone-chilling scream that echoed throughout the forest.

Partially blinded, it spiraled and careened down through the dense upper branches and crashed onto the sturdy lower limb of a large oak. Gilly struggled but could not twist free. "You vicious little creature!" it shrieked in rage. "To be blinded by such an insignificant nothing! I think I will just eat you here and be done with it. I should have preferred to take you to my lair for a more measured dissection and leisurely dining, but this will have to do."

It held Gilly tightly with one talon and the branch with the other, shaking her like a rag doll. It lifted and slammed her against the limb so that her head whipped against the hard wood. It was crushing the life from her. She gasped for breath.

The limb upon which the Wendigo had landed was about twenty feet in the air, safely above ground, it seemed. But the Wendigo had little knowledge of great cats or their ability to leap great distances. Had it known, it would have ascended quickly to a higher branch. Because suddenly, two avenging demons, Jami, the leopard, and Gar, the jaguar, scaled the tree in single bounds and were upon the Wendigo just as its cruel beak descended on Gilly's throat.

Gar's swift paw strike shattered the creature's neck and raked deep gouges across the Wendigo's head; his powerful jaws clamped upon its skull. Jamila was on its back, her fangs in its neck, raking with her hind claws until the Wendigo's scale-like feathers and flesh littered the ground beneath them. Shadow, the black panther, was just behind them, but there was no more room on the limb for him to join the melee. Fortunately, Jami and Gar were more than up to the task at hand.

Gilly could do little but wrap her arms about the tree limb and hold on for dear life in the commotion of the battle. She felt weak and was losing consciousness. The Wendigo clung to her body with its talons until it weakened from blood loss and toppled to the ground in a writhing death spasm. Even as it fell, it clutched at the girl and left deep raking wounds in her back

and side. Venom spewed through the air as it spiraled to the earth. Gar sprang down to the bloody snow to make sure of the creature's demise.

Gilly clung to the limb. "I'm here," said Jami. "It's all over." Gilly was bleeding from the deep scratches from the Wendigo's claws. Jami gently licked the wounds, as she would have done tending to any cub. "You ok, girl?"

Gilly did not answer.

"Shadow, help me!" cried Jami. "Gilly is unconscious. How do we get her down without injury? If she falls she will break her neck."

"Let her land on me," roared Max from below. "I will cushion her fall."

All the cats on the ground gathered round Max, who stood solidly below the limb. Shadow and Jami hooked their claws in Gilly's belt and lowered her as far as they could. Then they let her go. She landed squarely with a soft *whump* on Max's broad back. He did not flinch, for what is a hundred-pound girl to a five-hundred-pound African lion? A pittance. He gently lowered himself to the ground with the girl draped across his tawny shoulders.

She was barely breathing, and had not yet opened her eyes. "Gilly, Gilly," said Lola, licking her face. "Wake up, please wake up." Great mountain lion tears fell on the girl's face. She rolled her head to the side and groaned. Baptized by Lola's tears and her familiar voice, Gilly came back from the dark place of venom.

"What happened? What was that thing?"

"It was a bad dream, Gilly. Rest now," said Simone. "Let's get back to the campsite."

As Max gently rose with his precious burden, Boreas alighted on a nearby tree. He transformed to Ukpik in a whirlwind of snow and walked alongside the great cats. "I could not do this for her. It was a battle she needed to fight for herself," he said.

"And she is a sorceress of her own, it seems! Her magic was alien to the Wendigo; he underestimated this girl and her friends, eh?" He looked about proudly at all the cats. He laid his hand on Gilly's cheek and then her forehead. They walked back to the campsite, Gilly unmoving upon Max's back. A more formidable legion of guards was perhaps never seen in North America.

Ukpik built up the fire until it popped and roared and threw orange flames into the night sky. Gilly lay on a bough of pine needles that Ukpik had gathered. She began to move and then slowly opened her eyes, afraid of what she might see. Gladly, it was a multicolored ring of nine furry, whiskered muzzles, with bright, concerned eyes looking down at her from above. Lola's eyes were still wet. "You had us worried, Gilly," she purred.

Then the kind face of Ukpik leaned over her. He looked at the bloody, ivory tooth that still dangled from her necklace. "What is this?" he asked.

"It's a saltwater croc's tooth. My dad brought it back from Queensland, Australia. He gave it to me for good luck."

"Is the blood yours or the Wendigo's?"

"I don't know. After I stabbed the Wendigo with my knife and then lost it, I drove the croc's tooth into its eye as hard as I could. It was all I had . . . there were no other options. It was that thing or me!" Gilly was crying.

Ukpik patted her shoulder with his gnarled, calloused hand. "And very good luck it has been," said the shaman. "Such a talisman is an unknown and powerful medicine here in a place where no crocodile has ever set foot. Poor Wendigo! I almost feel sorry for the hideous beast. It didn't know what it was getting itself into when it set upon this young lady, eh, friends?"

Ukpik chuckled. "I must say that this is most certainly the first time a North American predator has been vanquished by the combined incisors of a South American jaguar, an African leopard, and an Australian saltwater crocodile. Yes, 'Old Windy' bit off a bit more than it could chew when it grabbed our Gilly."

He stood and uttered a fierce war cry into the night sky. He lifted his head and reached upward toward the heavens with his outstretched arms. "It is good to let your adversaries know that you have been victorious over a powerful foe, and to thank the ancestors who guided your success."

The cats all purred and growled mightily in agreement. Ukpik walked around the circle of cats. He scratched Jami and Gar behind their ears, where they could not reach, and said: "You did well to get there so quickly, my friends. You too, Shadow. And thank you, Max, for your strength to cushion her fall. Thank you all. No better guardians for this young woman could be imagined."

Then he cleaned the girl's wounds with warm water to remove the venom of the foul Wendigo, and applied a poultice that he made using moss gathered from the crevasse of a tree. He added a pinch of bone-colored powder to a cup of warm water and made her drink the broth. It was medicinal and anesthetic. The talons had torn her skin badly and her wounds needed to be sutured. Ukpik pulled a bone sewing needle from his shirt pocket and took his knife from his sheath. "Now I just need some suture material," he said, and looked about him. "What should we use? Catgut was once a common implement in hospitals," he said with a wink. "Perhaps hair would be a better option today!" He closed the ragged wounds with a series of neat stitches. "She will heal well but will carry these well-deserved scars of honor all her life." He tore apart strips from a pack cloth to fashion a swathe-like bandage.

Gilly felt no pain during the ministrations. When the procedure was over, she opened her eyes and muttered, "Thank you, Ukpik. Thank you." She was stiff, bruised, and exhausted from her ordeal. Ukpik gave her another cup of broth. The cats all circled round her and nuzzled her with their cold noses. She smiled wearily and lay back against Max's great flank. "What a night," she exclaimed, rolling her eyes and running her hands through her ginger-colored hair. "What was that thing, Ukpik?"

The shaman looked skyward for a moment, inhaled deeply the chill air, then spoke. "The Wendigo is a demon of the underworld and the subconscious that haunts the earth. It preys and feeds on doubt, uncertainty, and fear. It is a fierce and malevolent thing in its own right. Many a backwoods trapper, woodsman, and explorer have lost their lives and souls to the Wendigo. Simone knows the legends all too well. It is said to drag its victims through the forest so quickly that their feet catch fire, and they become mad. Then they are devoured. It always attacks at a time of great fatigue, weakness, or injury. You have defeated a great and powerful adversary, Gilly."

"I didn't do anything," said Gilly. "Jami and Gar killed it."

"You survived its attack! You fought it bravely, broke its hold on your spirit, and gave Jami and Gar the time and means to assist you," said Ukpik. "Know that your friends will always be a part of your courage and your truth. None of us endure without the help of our companions, our true friends. The strength of numbers will defeat any evil. The native people know the necessity of such cooperation," said the kind shaman. He smiled at Gilly. "Sleep now."

"I will keep the first watch," said Shadow, with a deep growl.

CHAPTER 30

DELIRIUM

In the morning, Ukpik was gone. By the light of day, Gilly examined her wounds. She had three long gashes, which the shaman had sutured, across her side and back from the Wendigo's talons. Ukpik had left a dollop of the poultice on a piece of birch bark with instructions that she apply it to the lacerations. She noticed the suture material that had closed her wounds was a mix of orange, black, and gold. She looked at the manes and fur of her companions, where irregular clumps seemed to be missing, most notably from Max's mane, Shadow's whiskers and tail, and Ravi's cheek. One by one she hugged them. "What would I do without you?" she asked. She was still feverish and felt quite weak, but she was eager to get on with the day.

"Today, you vill sit in the sled, and let us do ze work," said Sasha. And Gilly didn't argue. She ached all over and was dizzy if she stood or walked. She harnessed the cats to the traces and climbed into the sled. She pulled her down sleeping bag up around her neck and snuggled back against the wooden frame. It was a lovely day; the sun glinted brightly off the snow, and she felt like a princess on a tour through a magical wonderland. The cats followed Simone's lead and bounded down the trail. Gilly let the rhythm of their running lull her into a gentle repose. She closed her eyes and slept.

The cats ran with a graceful loping gait and a fluid rhythm. They had good weather and covered 165 miles. They reached Kaltag early in the day. In 1900, a measles epidemic had killed almost a third of its population. Passing through the desolate town, they left the Yukon River behind, as the trail turned west toward the coast. The team rested briefly in Unalakleet and then continued on past Shaktoolik to the abandoned coastal village of Ungalik. Before them, frozen into a corrugated grid of ice, was Reindeer Cove. The wide expanse of Norton Sound and the Bering Sea lay further beyond. In the far distance was Siberia.

Gilly awakened. She felt tired but renewed. She lifted herself from the sled and unharnessed the cats. She walked to the edge of the ice and looked out at the vast expanse of nothingness. Shadow and Lola stood on either side of her for support. She had an arm wrapped around each great neck, the mountain lion and the black panther, her old friends.

"Well, kid," said Shadow. "We've come a long way. I never thought we'd get this far."

"It's not over yet," added Lola. "We can't get overconfident or careless."

Gilly nodded. She was still recovering from her fever and delirium. "You are both right," she said.

"Let's all get some sleep," said Max. "I'll take the first watch tonight."

Gilly agreed. "We can assess the sea ice by the morning light. It is too dangerous to venture out in the dark. And we all need to rest!"

They had now journeyed 792 miles and were 206 miles from Nome. Once they crossed Norton Bay and reached Koyuk, they would be 171 miles from Nome. But the crossing of Norton Bay was to be an odyssey in its own right, as they would soon discover.

CHAPTER 31

NORTON BAY

In the morning, Gilly and her team arose and sat looking out across the bay. The ice along the shore seemed solid and intact. Out to the west, they could see the bright blue sea lap against the frozen shelf of ice. It was a sobering reminder of the potential consequences of leaving the relative safety of land.

Gilly knew the crossing from Ungalik across Norton Bay to the Koyuk Inlet was one of the most dangerous passages any musher would face. It was roughly thirty miles from Ungalik across the bay to Koyuk. Normally they could cover such a distance easily in several hours. But this was a treacherous passage. The sea ice that formed over the saltwater of Norton Sound was constantly shifting and agitated by the swelling sea beneath it. Great pressure ridges were formed in the ice when the plates buckled and were forced upwards by the sea. The brutal winds that howled across the flat expanse often caused large sections of the ice to break apart and drift out to sea.

When the wind blew from the west, it pushed the ice into the shore, but when it shifted and blew from the east, then the ice floes broke loose and were pushed seaward. Many a musher and his team, as well as hardened Eskimo hunters, had been lost when the ice broke up and drifted away from shore. A shift of several degrees on the compass in wind direction, or a delay of mere seconds, could seal one's fate. Some mushers chose to hug the shoreline for safety, although it cost them valuable time. Others risked everything and crossed the open expanse of sea ice, praying the Fates would treat them well.

The only way Gilly and the snowcats could catch the leaders was to risk crossing the ice on Norton Bay. It was just after sunrise, the sun beginning to peek over the horizon, as they prepared to venture onto the ice. Gilly made a final inspection through her binoculars. The ice appeared white and solid, with no channels of open water along the route. Dark ice was usually thin and rotten, a dangerous combination. Conditions today looked excellent, and Gilly was confident her faithful team could negotiate the crossing quickly and safely. She had to rely on their speed and light-footed grace.

As the cats guided the sled across the treacherous ice, Gilly still had the amulet around her neck. She grasped the empty pouch in her hand. "Please get us across safely," she whispered under her breath.

The cats had slowed their pace. No longer were they taking the long, bounding strides as they had on land, but were padding gently, as if on little cat feet, to lessen the impact.

When they were halfway across the bay, Gilly started to breathe easier. Although the wind was from the northeast, it was not blowing strongly at the moment. The cats were pulling smoothly, but their weight was far greater than that of any of the dog teams that had preceded them. Still, it seemed they were going to be lucky. The sun was rising and would soon soften the ice. In the distance, Gilly could make out the tracks leaving the ice and leading back up onto solid ground. Now they were nearly three-quarters of the way across. Koyuk was in sight. They would soon reach solid ground.

Suddenly, there was a loud boom followed by a cracking

sound, and a blue line appeared between the team and the shoreline. It was a seam of water where the ice had split in half. The slab of ice was breaking away! The cats halted and looked back at Gilly. In the early-morning light, they could see their dire predicament.

"Now what, Princess?" asked Lola.

"Curses!" said Gar.

They were suddenly adrift on an ice floe the size of a baseball diamond infield.

"What do we do?" said Gilly. "Ukpik, only you can save us now."

High in a conifer on the shoreline, unseen by Gilly and her cats, the snowy owl sat watching with interest. But he did not fly to them. He only watched and waited.

Gilly sat down beside the sled. All the cats had gathered to the center of the ice floe to keep it from tilting to the right or left. Although the floe seemed to be stable enough, it was definitely drifting out to sea. All seemed lost.

"It was good while it lasted, wasn't it?" said Lola to Shadow.

"Yes, dear, it was."

Gar growled. "I've swum many rivers and lakes in my day. It's what we jaguars do. But this water is too cold. And we cannot leave Gilly."

"I fear we are now truly lost," said Gilly in a sad, forlorn voice.

As she spoke, the ice floe seemed to hit a reef or obstruction of some sort, and stopped drifting out to sea. The waves began to lap against the now stationary slab of ice.

"What happened?" asked Ravi.

"I don't know. We must be hung up on something," said Gilly.

"Here in the middle of the bay? What could cause us to stop?"

"Not what, but who!" said a voice from the far side of the floe.

The cats and Gilly all looked curiously toward the seaward

side of the floe, where a long, spear-like object rose from the water towards them.

"My God, what is it?" said Che, for he had never seen such a thing.

"Oh my gosh," shouted Gilly excitedly. "It looks like a narwhal!"

"A what?" said the cats in unison.

"A narwhal! They have a lone single tooth that grows amazingly long into a unicornish tusk."

"But unicorns are mythical. Are these so-called narwhals fierce? It looks most dangerous!" said Jami.

"Oh, never fear," said the narwhal, who had emerged from beneath the edge of the floe so that his eyes were above the waterline. His tusk was over six feet long. "My name is Nigel," he said.

"Now that you mention it," pondered Gilly, "narwhals don't normally live in these waters. You are usually on the Atlantic side near Greenland, aren't you?"

"Well, yes, actually, yer right, lass. But, as you may well know, global warming is causing our glaciers to melt. My friends and I, we call ourselves a pod like most whales, decided to come explore the western side of the continent. So we just swam over the Arctic ice cap via the North Pole . . . and there you have it. But to get to the crux of the matter," said a perplexed Nigel, "what are *you* doing floating here in the bay with these enormous cats? A narwhal on the wrong side of the pond is not so unusual. Lions and tigers on an ice floe in the Bering Sea? I have never heard of such a thing."

Nigel was abruptly joined by a blubbery old walrus with bristle whiskers. Nigel turned to his fellow flippered marine mammal. "Winston, have you ever seen such a spectacle as this? Lions, tigers, and leopards on an ice floe bobbing in the Bering Sea?" The walrus hooked his two-foot-long ivory tusks over the edge of the ice floe to rest.

"Not in my lifetime," he sighed, hanging vertically in the water while they chatted.

"Actually," said Nigel, "now that you mention it, I talked to a Minke whale a couple of months ago who heard from a gray whale migrating across the far Pacific about a Hindi boy and a Bengal tiger floating in a lifeboat down by Mexico. But that was just *one* big cat. Here we have, let's see, one, two, three, four, five, six, seven, eight, *nine* oversized felines, not to mention one red-haired girl, bobbing on this ice floe."

Looking up at Gilly, Winston fidgeted his whiskers three or four times, sniffled twice and snorted once. He rolled his ping-pong-sized eyes and looked at the cats with a befuddled expression on his pudgy face. "Just what is going on here, anyway?"

"We are racing in the Iditarod," said Gilly with exasperation. "But the ice broke away and now we are drifting out to sea. Every second we lose puts us further behind the other competitors. Not to mention we could be blown completely across the Bering Sea to Siberia!"

"Yes, well, I must say you don't look like the typical dogsled team we usually see in these waters. You aren't trying to pull the wool over my eyes, are you?" said Winston with a tilt of his head.

"No, no!" shouted Gilly. "We are entered in the Iditarod, but, well, they're cats instead of dogs. But we can still win!"

"You're not going to do that floating out into the Bering Sea, my dear," replied Nigel.

"Yes, I know," said Gilly sadly. "Can you help us?"

"What do you think, Winston?" said Nigel with a questioning look.

"That is an interesting question. And one that no dogsledding team has ever asked me," said the leathery walrus, who looked rather like a comfortable reading chair with ivory walking sticks. "Yes, I think we can help you. It is Nome you seek?"

"Yes," replied Gilly. "We need to get across to Koyuk Inlet, then to Baldhead and Isaac's Point. We are retracing the last parts of the route that the rescuers followed to bring the diphtheria vaccine to the needy children."

"A noble thing," said Winston. "A noble venture, indeed. Let us see what we can do about getting you back closer to shore. Summon all flippered marine mammals to the fray, Nigel!"

Nigel dipped beneath the water, and soon there was a sharp blowing and whistling sound. Promptly there was an echoing whistle. Then another. And another. And another. A pod of narwhals rose from the waters of the bay. A pair of Minke whales, a solitary humpback whale, three all-white beluga whales, five seals of various species, a sea lion, and Winston's brothers, a pair of mustachioed walruses, appeared at the windward edge of the ice floe.

"We need to help this young lady and her feline companions get back to shore so they can beat some dogs at their own game. This is payback for all the years of yipping and yapping along the shoreline while we were trying to rest."

"Say what?" said the larger of the walruses, who was hard of hearing.

"We need to push this ice floe back to shore!" said Nigel emphatically.

"Oh, why didn't you say so?" replied the beautiful all-white beluga. "No problemo. Let's do it, gang! One, two, three, push! One, two, three, push!"

Together, the whales, seals, walruses, and narwhals pushed and pushed until the ice floe began to move. Gradually it slid against the waves and slipped towards shore.

CHAPTER 32

A TALL BLACK FIN

Without warning, a six-foot-tall black fin emerged from the water just beyond the floe, coming at them rapidly. "Oh no!" cried Gilly. "Look out! Killer whales!" But before she could finish her warning, a pod of four black-and-white orcas had encircled the floe. One of the two juvenile orcas rose beneath the seals and flipped a seal named Monk into the air like a toy.

"Wow, it's like a smorgasbord a la mer," shouted the other young orca.

The second juvenile orca caught the terrified seal on his nose and was preparing to eat it when Gilly cried out, "Stop right now! We be of one blood, ye and I. We ask safe passage from our kindred spirits of the sea!"

The two juvenile orcas looked perplexed. The adult male and female rose, noses out of the water, and looked at the menagerie of cats, the ruddy-cheeked young girl on the ice floe, and the marine mammals pushing them to shore. It was an odd situation, to be sure.

"Who said that?" said the large male orca sternly. "Who asks for 'safe passage,' for a pardon, as it were, from dinner?"

"I did," said Gilly bravely, in a loud voice. And she said again: "We be of one blood, ye and I. By the law of all that is right and good in the world. And by the Law of the Jungle . . . and the Law of the Pack!"

"Who are you, a two-legged, finless pipsqueak, to invoke the sacred Law of the Wild? I have not been so challenged in years. 'Right and good' have little currency in the wild when hunger or survival is at stake. Now law and justice, that's another issue. Speak! Who are you?"

"My name is Gilly Wells and I live in Anchorage, Alaska," said Gilly. "I know you are the lords of the sea and of this bay, but I beg you to let my friends pass safely. We are on a quest, racing in the Iditarod."

"Where did you learn the sacred shibboleth? The bequest to grant safe passage?"

"I learned it in a book by Kipling," said Gilly. "It was the secret oath of the jungle that the wise bear Baloo taught Mowgli to gain passage from the masters of each animal's domain." Gilly had memorized these phrases from reading the stories over and over.

"What do you say, sir?" she asked bravely. "Is there still honor in the clan of the sea wolves? I hope you will show more civility than your four-legged wolf cousins of the forest."

"Those flea-bitten curs are no kin of ours!" said the male orca.

"Someday, perhaps, if we have a chance to meet again, I can return a favor to you, Great Orca," said Gilly.

"What could you possibly do for me? Or for my kind?" he asked with a smirk. "Give me a tub in a zoo and teach me to do somersaults for herring? I performed tricks for frozen fish in the San Diego Zoo for three years before I escaped with my cousin Willy. Trust me, I won't be returning any day soon!"

"I am sorry for all that. Perhaps I could someday remove a hook, a harpoon, help you escape from a net, or better yet, lead a political advocacy group that works to preserve your freedom, your habitat, and the sea!"

"She is persuasive, isn't she, dear," said the big male to

his mate.

"Yes," she replied, "This red-haired thing is clearly *The One* that Ukpik mentioned. Bah, she wouldn't even be a morsel of sushi, and if we ate those cats we'd be picking fur out of our teeth for weeks."

"On this rare occasion," said the male orca, "I am happy to honor your request, young lady. It is a rare thing to encounter one who has learned the Law of the Pack, or Pod, as the case may be, and respects the Code of the Wild, whether it be jungle, mountain, or sea."

In the background, the two young orcas had continued to toss the petrified seal, Monk, back and forth on their noses.

"It is highly contrary to the demands of our appetite, but I think today we might just be able to hunt a bit further out to sea. I have heard that the mackerel and tuna are running well closer to the Siberian coast anyway, eh, dear? And there is less chance of mercury poisoning," the big male orca said with a toothy grin. "Let's go, boys. Put the seal back on the floe. We will find a fatter one for you on the Kamchatka coast."

As the four orcas swam away, the young seal lay gasping on the ice floe, his eyes still white with terror. "Look, Monk," said Winston the Walrus, "it is a short life and yer a long-time dead. You have been given a rare reprieve. That doesn't happen very often in this great wide sea. The predator-prey cycle is our life. We all die at some point. This would have been as good a day as any; but tomorrow is a far better option, eh, my friend? Come on, bucko, let's get moving."

With that, the narwhals, seals, walruses, and whales all pushed and pushed against the ice floe until it once again slipped toward shore. In time they had moved the floe back to the ragged seam of ice from which it had broken free. When the ice shelves touched, Gilly's team was ready and sprang across from the unstable ice floe to the solid land ice. Once safe, they turned and faced their rescuers.

"Oh, how can we thank you?" cried Gilly.

"You can run for all of us!" sang out Nigel. "Be safe and know that our thoughts and prayers go with you and your noble snowcats." All the other whales, seals, and walruses whistled, snorted, grunted, harrumphed, blew spume from their blowholes, and slapped their tails on the surface to say good-bye. Tails and tusks dipped beneath the surface.

The humpback whale rose out of the water before them with her rostrum, or nose, upward. Her underbelly was a dazzling white that contrasted with the brilliant blue water when she turned to her side. Her great eye was level with the floe, and Gilly and the cats stood looking at her, eyeball to eyeball. "Stay out of trouble, Bubble!" she chortled, diving into the sea. Her great tail hung over them for a second, and then the great flukes rolled gently beneath the water, sending a fine shower of droplets into the air. She was gone.

"Holy camoly. And they are all really mammals? Zounds!" said Max.

High above them, Boreas hooted his "chissssschchchkakaka" and gazed at the spectacle.

CHAPTER 33

THE WHITE BEAR

Once on solid land, the cats were eager to start off again, but Gilly insisted that they rest, melt snow for water, and reassess their strategy for the race. They had made it safely across Norton Bay, but still had 171 miles of forbidding Alaskan terrain and wilderness to negotiate. Just ahead lay the steep ascent up Little McKinley. Beyond that was the daunting trail to Golovin, then Bluff and Port Safety, before reaching Nome.

Gilly built a fire and made the cats lie before it to dry their paws and fur. They had all gotten their feet wet on the ice floe when the waves had washed over the ice. She carefully examined each animal's paws for any injury. She removed clumps of frozen ice wedged between their toes that might cause irritation. Then she rubbed their pads and toes with balm. Her father had taught her how important it was to care for one's team. They were her lifeblood and deserved the best she could give them. It was an essential part of the pact of respect and caring between the team and the musher.

As they relaxed around the campfire drying their paws, a booming voice said, "You've done well to get this far!" Gilly and the cats looked up with alarm. The cats sniffed the air and were frustrated to find no scent. Slightly downwind and northwest of their camp was a large snow berm where the ice had buckled into the landmass of the beach, creating an ice wall some ten feet high. The voice came from behind the jagged ridge of ice.

"We should have done better surveillance before we stopped to rest," whispered Simone, alert to whatever or whomever was on the other side of the ice wall.

"Requesting permission to enter your campsite," said the voice, which was deep and rumbling.

"If you come in peace," said Gilly, "we welcome you . . . whoever you are."

A pair of white ears with black tips rose above the top of the ice ridge. Then two black eyes and a black nose, big teeth, a white furry neck, shoulders, back, chest, haunches, legs, arms, paws, claws, and nubby tail of a full-grown polar bear!

"Wow," muttered Jamila. "Never seen one of those before!"

"That is one big dude!" muttered Che.

"Welcome to the northern wild, my feline friends. And you too, Miss Gilly."

"How did you know?" Gilly started to ask, then said, "Oh, Ukpik, or Boreas, told you we were coming, right?"

"Yes. I hear that you met the Wendigo and survived. You are a brave young woman. And I was watching your escapade on the bay. A bit of a worry there, eh? I am a darn good swimmer myself, as you may know, but not much I could have done to help you in that predicament. Good thing Nigel, Winston and their flippered pals were up to the task. And fortunately Blackie was in a pleasant mood today. He is revered by Ukpik's clan, you know. The orca is in the sea what my bear clan is here on land to the native people. We give and we take."

"What are you anyway?" asked Jamila, who had never seen such a huge white creature. "Are you an albino? I thought all the bears in Alaska were hibernating during the winter."

"Not polar bears, *ursus maritimus*, my spotted friend. My name is Oolab. The native people call me nanuq, nanook, or nanuuk."

"Wow," said Jami. "We have white leopards too but they are pretty rare. Shadow is really a black leopard even though he is known as a panther. It's all in the pigment, eh?"

"I didn't know that," said Lola. "Aren't you something special!" she said, winking at the dark one.

"We have a common bond, you know," said Oolab. "When the ancient glacial ice bridge connected Asia to North America, our ancestors roamed freely across this land. Our forbearer species, giant cats including saber-toothed tigers, bears, and woolly mammoths, all once lived here. The four-legged wolf-like canines were scavengers, an afterthought, like hyenas, dingoes, coyotes, and later, dogs. We bears and cats were the lords of this land. So really, you are returning royalty!"

The cats all sat up proudly, puffing out their chests at the praise.

"We are honored by your words," said Max. "It seems we truly do have a common lineage that goes back to the ice age. You have remained, while we strayed to the far corners of the earth. But I speak for all my fellow cats who sit before you when I say: We be of one blood, ye and I."

Oolab sat looking at his new friends through his great black eyes. His paws were resting in his lap. He didn't have many companions in this vast crystalline desert. He imagined a different time when they might have roamed this wild northern land together. He sniffed. "I am at your service."

"Thank you for your kind words, Oolab, but we do have a race to run and time is fleeting." Simone had become their taskmaster and was intent on keeping distractions to a minimum.

"Exactly!" said Oolab, rising from the ground. "And that's why I'm here. I have never been to Nome, but I've gotten close.

Too close, actually. Too many guns and people who want a white fur rug for their cabin floor, so I stay as far from civilization as I can. Why, just yesterday morning, a burly black-bearded musher took two potshots at me as he crossed the beach to the mountain trail. He was whipping his dogs feverishly."

"I am sorry," said Gilly. "That would be Mean Zeke. He is not the best example of our kind. So he is a full day ahead of us? He must have less than a hundred miles to go by now."

"Survival is one thing," replied Oolab. "The native people have always understood that relationship. They revere and honor any animal they kill to survive. We are all part of a greater existence, you see. Humph. Such is life in the wild . . . and the not-so-wild. Anyway, you have a steep climb up the side of Little McKinley. Be careful and don't get going too fast coming down or the sled can flip off the trail. Once you get out to Elim and Port Safety you can turn it loose, and if you are lucky, you can catch that mangy dog whipper. Give him a cuff for me if you do, eh?"

"Why do you help us, Oolab?" said Shadow.

"I honor Ukpik, the shaman, and I admire the dream vision that brought Gilly to this quest. And you cats are a link to my heritage." His black eyes glittered like opals in the sunlight. "Here, climb on my shoulder and I will stand up so you can scout the trail beyond the ice ridge."

Gilly clambered up on Oolab, and when he stood, her feet were nearly eight feet in the air.

"See how the path goes behind the large boulder? Your friend Zeke made a false trail to the left to throw any followers off course. Go right, into the ravine, and behind the hillside. Then you will find the true path."

"You are a good friend and we are fortunate to have met you!" said Max.

"Sometimes you make your own fortune by the brave

choices you make. You set the heavens in motion," said the great bear.

"I am glad ve are on same side," said Ravi to Sasha. "He one big boy!"

"Walk softly and carry a big paw!" said Lola with a scrunch of her whiskers.

There was a flutter of wing beats. Boreas settled on a nearby pine branch.

"Ah, greetings, wise Ukpik," said Oolab with a bow.

"Good day to you, noble Oolab!" keened Boreas. "I see you have met Ms. Wells and her noble companions," he said, rotating his head 180 degrees as he looked first at the bear and then at Gilly and then the nine imposing felines. And he smiled, if owls can be said to smile, for surely his eyes sparkled. "How is your side, girl?"

"Ok," Gilly replied. "I'm still stiff but getting better every day."

"Good. But now you must go. I have been on a reconnaissance flight over the mountain. The way is difficult and the time is short. Zeke is halfway to Nome as we speak."

"Boreas," asked Gilly, "I worry about the finish. What if someone is afraid of the snowcats? What if someone has a gun and shoots at them like Zeke shot at Oolab?"

"I will be watching over you," replied the owl. "You have been sufficiently resourceful so far. You are wise to consider all possibilities. Know that it will all shake out in the end. The Fates dictate all!"

Gilly hitched the cats into the traces. "Good-bye, Oolab," she cried. One by one, the great cats said the same to their distant brother.

"We be of one blood..." he growled after them with a catch in his voice, for displays of affection are an uncommon thing among grown polar bears.

CHAPTER 34

WEST WITH THE NIGHT

The veil of night was again descending. As they neared the land bridge to Siberia, once called Beringia, the cats felt a strange stirring in their bones. They were not strangers to this land. They thought of the tales Oolab had told them. Their ancestors had crossed the once-frozen ice bridge from Russia to North America long ago, along with ancient bison, woolly mammoths, oxen, moose, and other prehistoric animals. This was no foreign land to the snowcats of the northern wild. They, not the domesticated sled dogs, were the primordial ones who had first inhabited this land long ago. At that time a sheet of ice covered much of the world in what was known as the Pleistocene Epoch. Glaciers extended from Patagonia to the Yukon and from Tasmania to Asia. Their ancestors had roamed freely across this domain. These snowcats were the true Ancient Ones, and they were coming home.

Gilly guided the team carefully along the trail. They kept a steady pace but did not overrun the path. Gilly was cautious when she needed to be and let the cats choose their time to run swiftly. They saw the false trail Zeke had set to delay and confuse his competitors. Gilly turned the team to the right and they ascended Little McKinley with no problems. The night was dark but still. The blizzard and winds of the earlier days seemed spent, the trail was good, and they were able to make up for lost time.

Gilly & the Snowcats

Many Iditarod dogsled drivers would later exclaim that they had seen visions that night. It was a common thing for mushers to hallucinate when deprived of sleep in the wilderness. But these claims seemed different. Some mushers had the same vision of a demon team of giant beasts that bounded past them at blinding speed, roaring, snarling, and caterwauling, with a small waif behind them in the sled singing something that one musher said sounded like "Grizzled Castles Spool." Later, another musher described the oath more distinctly as "Girls and Cats Rule!" He couldn't understand what it meant, but concluded, with a sober nod, that it was time to hang up his racing bib.

CHAPTER 35

THE LAST MILES

They had stopped for a brief rest. Gilly checked all the harnesses and secured the gear in her sled. The moon rose over the whiteness of the snowy expanse that lay before them. Some hundred miles away the finish waited. Mean Zeke seemed destined for another win. Simone looked back at her harness mates, the first cats to ever run the Iditarod. She looked at the girl, the young woman, Gilly Wells, who stood beside the small sled, waiting expectantly. Although the smallest of the cats, Simone still led the team; her feet floated on the snow crust and she could sense the path that allowed the bigger cats to gain maximum purchase without sinking deeply into the snow.

"I think it iz ze time for us to show thez doggies what a real team, a team of bona fide felines, can do, eh?" She winked a sly smile and kicked a bit of snow onto Gar and Jamila. "We have a full moon to guide us and precious cargo to keep, my friends." Simone looked fondly at Gilly. "Shall we go?"

Each cat in turn murmured its rumbling, throaty reply of "Grrrrrrrrooowwl!"

With the dusk descending, the cats began to walk, then trot, then lope, faster than any normal beast. To any who might have been watching, the collection of progenitor cats, of the veldt, the mountains, and the jungle, were fierce, regal, and powerful

Gilly & the Snowcats

beyond imagination. Steadily, they lengthened their stride, longer and faster, until they were racing across the snowy trail like wraiths of the night. The runners of the sled hissed and began to melt the snow beneath it. Later followers would comment on the appearance of scorched earth where the snow had melted down to the ground. Such was the friction and heat of their passage. A smoky plume of steam, melting snow, and burnt earth drifted into the air behind them.

Gilly was overwhelmed with sleep deprivation and fatigue. She was still feverish, and the jagged wounds on her side ached and burned. Any bending or twisting caused pain, and blood oozed through her bandages. She barely clung to the sled. Her hands were cold and cramped. Her fingers and knuckles were blistered and raw from the cold and the constant gripping. Still they raced on.

In the early dawn, Gilly could make out the silhouette of a large man and his baying team of Siberian huskies racing down the trail. Beyond him in the distance lay the faintly lit skyline of Nome. It was Mean Zeke bearing down on the finish line with less than five miles to go. Zeke had seen the shadow of his follower closing and was prepared to do anything to preserve his lead.

Yet it was uncanny: the following team seemed to surge across the snowfield. They were a massive and powerful team, unlike anything he had ever seen. He marveled at their speed even as he despised them. Their grace and elegance was incomparable. He hated them more profoundly than he had ever hated any opponent. He threw large thumbtacks and looped knots of bailing wire—which could tighten dangerously around paws—onto the trail behind him. His opponents sidestepped the wire and the tacks effortlessly. The pursuing team drew down on Zeke.

Zeke felt hot breath on his neck and, turning, saw the fierce snarling faces of Gilly's nine cats of the glacial wild. He had no explanation for what he saw. There was a lion, a jaguar, a puma, a black panther, a cheetah, a leopard, a lynx, a tiger, and a snow leopard. He was petrified. His dogs had smelled the odor of cat and had their hackles up anticipating an easy meal. Now, they too were frightened beyond understanding.

"Who are you?" snarled Zeke.

"Gilly Wells!" she shouted and saw the look of disbelief on his ugly face.

"You don't belong here!" he shouted in a fierce, angry voice. "This is a race for grown men, not little girls. I will crush you like I should have crushed your father."

Fuming with indignation, Zeke pulled a whip from his sled and slashed at his opponent, the unthinking reflex of an evil man. The end of the whip split the skin on Gilly's cheek. It burned in the night air and blood ran down her neck. Zeke snapped his whip again and struck Gilly on the hand, causing her to lose her grip on the sled. She fell, tumbling headlong in the snow while the cats lurched forward. Sensing the change in weight, Simone backed the team down and turned them to where Gilly lay stunned in the snow. She had been knocked senseless by the force of her fall. The team gathered round.

"Gilly! Gilly, are you okay?" asked Lola.

Gilly's eyes seemed to roll in her head. Slowly her vision came back into focus. Her faithful cats, still harnessed together, were in a semicircle around her. "Where is Zeke?"

The cats looked over toward Nome and the finish line.

"We have a race to win!" groaned Gilly. She dragged herself to her feet and grabbed onto the back of the sled. "Let's go! Hiya, snowcats! Hiya!"

The cats bounded forward with such power that the sled whipped wildly from right to left. It was all Gilly could do to hold on to the careening frame as they bore down on the other team. Although it seemed like an eternity, they soon were pulling up

alongside Zeke's sled. He looked at them with an amazed but brutish scowl. His dogs were foaming and near exhaustion. The sight of the giant snowcats brought whimpers of fear from the entire team. "Go away!" screamed Zeke. "You don't belong here!" Then he snapped the whip again, this time hitting Max on his shoulder as the cats pulled abreast of Zeke's dogs. The sting provoked a mighty roar that shook the night.

Max retaliated and cuffed Zeke's lead dog aside as a kitten might bat a ball of catnip. The team was thrown sideways off the trail and tumbled in a chaotic tangle of harness, dogs, sled, and gear to the bottom of the embankment. Yelps, whimpers, and raging curses colored the air. Gilly stopped her cats to look down at the man's crumpled dogsled team. Zeke was holding his arm tightly to his side. His right shoulder had been dislocated in the tumult of the crash. Blood ran from his nostrils and from a gash on his head. He bellowed like a bull, angry and terrified for the first time in his life.

"I am not just a little girl, Mr. Meaner. I am me! Gilly Wells, the only daughter of Gil and Kate Wells. We are all what we choose to be. And I sure wouldn't choose to be you! These are the snowcats of the northern wild! Despite your treachery, we just beat you, fair and square, at your own game. *Hasta la vista*, Mean Zeke!"

One by one, the cats roared in solidarity. It was a sound that echoed in Zeke's ears for the rest of his life. The roar reverberated in the otherwise still night air. Far away, people looked up and wondered.

Gilly and the snowcats raced across the remaining flat, barren landscape towards Nome. It was only a few miles to town and the finish line on Front Street. They left the humiliated man and his dogs yelping along the trail. Zeke lay stunned beneath his overturned sled.

CHAPTER 36

NOME

Now Gilly could see the outline of the town of Nome. Two giant wood pillars supported a burled log inscribed with the words: "End of Iditarod Sled Dog Race." As she approached the finish line, she could discern burly, bearded men in bulky orange snowmobile suits milling about at the finish line. A white banner was emblazoned with red block letters reading "FINISH" and gaudy multicolored sponsorship logos. The temperature was 5 degrees Fahrenheit, typical for that time of year.

Moments later, as the sun broke the horizon, the cats felt the magic of the shaman beginning to wane. Their gait slowed, and one by one they transformed back into their normal selves. Simone became a slightly smaller Simone, but was now the largest of the cats. Max, Gar, Che, Ravi, Sasha, Shadow, Lola, and Jamila once again reverted to normal size. Gilly ran beside the sled as they approached the finish line. There were bright lights and cameras. An announcer was shouting that Zeke Meaner seemed to have crashed and that an upstart team was now coming across the finish line. Was it Aliy Zirkle?

Gilly and the cats dashed across the line and down Front Street to stunned silence. An official darted out onto the street. The man grabbed Gilly's sled handlebars and shouted, "What the heck are you doin'? We got the lead finisher for the Iditarod coming in a few

minutes."

"I am the leader. I'm the winner!" shouted Gilly.

"We got no record of a #66 or a #99 stopping at any of the checkpoints on this race!" he shouted.

"Don't yell at me," said Gilly. "Your checkpoints were already closed at the first four stops, and quite honestly I was afraid you would hurt my cats at the others, so I just didn't stop. It was an 'executive decision' as my mom would say! We were going too fast anyway," she said with a wry smile. She looked unapologetically at the disbelieving, red-faced man.

"Ain't no way you won this race, young lady!" he hollered.

"Yes, actually, we did!" Gilly exclaimed proudly.

"You can't be serious! Git off the course before I have you arrested. This here is a dogsled race. Says so right on the banner. D. O. G. Dog! As in canine. Woof woof. Ya git it?"

"Well, you need to change the rules," she said.

Several other officials crowded around Gilly and the yapping official. "Oscar, get this girl and her kitty cats out of the finish chute, now!"

Meanwhile, in the confusion, another sled team, mushed by Aliy Zirkle, had slipped past Zeke's team in the final stretch, beating him by twenty-two seconds. It was a stunning victory for Zirkle and a demoralizing defeat for Zeke. Gilly glowed knowing that even though she hadn't gotten the credit for the win with her cats, at least a woman would be on the top of the podium. It made her heart happy!

Mean Zeke and his team stumbled across the finish line, exhausted, bloodied, and stunned by their humiliating experience in the final stretch of the race. Zeke held his dislocated arm tightly against his side and grimaced with every movement. He glowered at Gilly and her team as they pranced down the street.

The dogs sensed a new advantage and pulled forward to

attack the team of cats. As they approached, the cats turned in mass toward the surging canines, arched their backs, eyes blazing, and growled in unison with a guttural, primal sound that put the dogs back on their haunches. The look in the cats' eyes reminded the dogs that these were not normal felines, and that they had the potential of a fearful transformation. The dogs began whining and yelping and flipped the sled backwards, despite Zeke's shouting and curses. He lay groaning and cursing on the ground, his arm pointing in the wrong direction.

Zeke looked up and saw the sign outside Chilkoot Charlie's Bar: "We cheat the other guy and pass the savings on to you!" Something in his dazed brain caused him to think, "That don't seem fair." And then he passed out.

CHAPTER 37

THE JOURNEY'S END

A post with a wooden arrow pointing in various directions of the compass stood at the end of the street. London: 4376 miles. Siberia: 164 miles. Miami: 4475 miles. Seattle: 1968 miles. Los Angeles: 2871 miles. Beyond was an old white church with an illuminated cross atop its steeple. The Gold Dust Saloon was at the end of the street.

From the back of the crowd, a tall man in a fur robe walked toward Gilly and led her and the cat team to a back alley where they could collect themselves. "Come with me," said Ukpik. Several of his tribal members shouldered onlookers out of the way and protected the girl's team from shouting bystanders and assorted curs. Once they were in a quiet place, Ukpik looked down at her and smiled. "You did it! All alone and with grace and courage. All of you should be very proud!"

"But we won, and they won't give us credit for winning the race," said Gilly sadly.

"Does it really matter what these officials in orange suits say? What matters is that you ran the race and you won! You know that and your team knows that. I know that." Ukpik smiled at her and helped push the sled down the street.

"We couldn't have done it without you, Ukpik," she said softly.

"Ah, but you did. You summoned the necessary strength. I did not make you something you weren't. Your dream was just the right size. The adventure of your life is just beginning. I am happy for you all. But now we need to get you home. It is a long drive, but we have good company!"

Ukpik's wife of many years, Evening Star, rode with them. She had dark, piercing eyes and her voice was gentle, like the wind caressing the treetops on a summer night. She wore a long dress of earth-tone taffeta and muslin. She had dream-catcher hoop earrings and a necklace with a finely carved piece of scrimshaw around her neck. She was a radiant woman, kind and confident. She told them stories of her girlhood growing up along the wild Alaskan coast, of running with caribou, swimming with the fur seals, and flying with the snow geese on their long migrations.

Gilly absorbed everything that Evening Star said. She did not doubt one word of her marvelous tales. She was an Athabaskan Scheherazade with tales of adventure and marvel and mystery.

After they had driven for many miles, there was a yowling from the back of the truck. Ukpik pulled the vehicle over. They were back in the Yentna region along a deserted section of road. It was in a thickly forested area near where they had camped the second night, and where they had been attacked by Hugh the Wolverine. Simone leapt from the back of the old truck bed.

"We are back in my neck of the woods now," she said. "It was a great joy for me to run with you, my friends. I hope we meet again!" One by one, the cats all said good-bye to Simone.

Gilly put her arms around Simone's wild furry neck and felt whiskers on her wet cheeks. "Good-bye, Simone!" she cried. The lynx bounded across a drift of snow, lighter than air, her feet seeming to float above the surface. In mid-leap, Simone looked back and winked, disappearing into the sun-dappled forest.

"Vat a cat!" said Ravi. Sasha looked at him with a slightly cocked eyebrow. "Hmmm," was all she said.

They traveled in silence for many miles before the sadness of Simone's departure faded. It was time to sleep, and for many miles there was no sound from the back of the truck. Gilly's head leaned against the window. Ukpik and Evening Star rode in silence, though they seemed to communicate wordlessly throughout the journey with glances and the touch of fingertips.

CHAPTER 38

HOME AT LAST

Finally, on the afternoon of the next day, the tires of the old truck crunched over the gravel driveway of the Wells property. The old barn stood just as they had left it ten days before, yet all seemed changed. The house was quiet. Gilly's parents had not yet returned from their travels.

Old Bolo limped down the steps toward the gathered cats. He looked towards them with his rheumy eyes. "Arrrouuuuu!" he howled into the sky. "Word travels fast. I never should have underestimated you, dear girl. And you too, cats! You have made us all proud."

Gilly pushed the barn doors open wide. Mice and rats scrambled everywhere. The cats, bedraggled and sleepy, looked at the scurrying rodents with disinterest. "I'm too tired to chase them," said Lola. They all nodded as one.

"Later!" muttered Che.

"Yeah," said Max.

"Si, mañana!" said Gar.

Ukpik and Evening Star stood patiently beside the truck. "How can I, can we, ever thank you?" asked Gilly.

"You have thanked us more than you know," said Ukpik. "Whatever you do, Gilly, continue to do it with all your heart and soul. Live joyfully, yet with reverence. In doing so, you honor all existence." Gilly hugged them both. Ukpik and Evening Star scratched the cats behind all sixteen of their ears!

"Good-bye. Good-bye!" Gilly shouted as they drove from the yard. "Every time I see a snowy owl, I will think of you!"

"Don't worry, we will see each other again," said Ukpik.

"Please say hello to Simone, Oolab, Nigel, Winston, Castor, Moose and all our friends!" she shouted. And then they were alone again.

"Well," said Gilly, finally breaking the silence, "what will we do for our next adventure? We can fix the barn up and all live here together forever!"

She looked at the cats, who lay sprawled on bales of hay or on the barn floor. They were uneasy and somewhat agitated, but Gilly didn't seem to notice at first.

"Gilly," said Sasha softly. "Ravi and I are going back to Asia . . . to the Himalayas. It is in our blood, our bones. It is our home and where we belong. You understand."

She did and she didn't. But she loved them no matter what. Gilly hugged them with tears on her cheeks. They left the next morning, sneaking down to the wharf and slipping aboard a Russian freighter headed for the Kamchatka Peninsula.

Then Jamila and Che announced their plan to return to the land of their roots: Africa. They figured they'd catch a ride to Miami and then slip aboard a container boat back to Kenya or Tanzania. Gilly hugged them and watched them leave, her speedy golden cats of the veldt, as they sauntered down the path with their sleek lines and graceful loping gait.

Then it was Gar's turn. Her brave, rippling jaguar, who, with Jami, had killed the Wendigo, was headed back to his native Amazon basin.

"What will we do without you, Gar, without all of you?" asked Gilly.

"Just be happy, lil' sister," said Gar. "You've got the world by the tail, ya know? Yer in our hearts forever."

Gilly & the Snowcats

"Vija con Dios, Gar!" whispered Gilly. And he sprang over the bushes and was gone.

Finally, the day after that, Max announced his plan to jump a train heading down to Saskatoon. He was bound for the east coast, for Maine, to see his kin. Gilly hung about his great neck. "I'll miss you an awful lot," she whispered to him. "You were the first to join us and you were the king of my beasts, Max. You kept us together."

"But you brought us together, Gilly," said Max. "And Ukpik let us live a dream! You are my favorite two-leg, Gilly," he said in a scratchy voice. Then he whispered good-bye and ambled down the trail behind the barn, past the bushes where he first watched Lola and Shadow pulling Gilly on the sled. He turned and smiled, then jumped up on the stone fence that circled the yard, turned once, and was gone.

Gilly, Lola, and Shadow sat forlornly on a bale of hay. "Once we were nine; ten, including me," said Gilly. "The most resourceful, powerful, and fastest team to ever run the Iditarod!"

"And best looking!" added Lola.

"Honestly, I never thought we could do it," said Shadow. "I didn't believe till the end. Until after everyone else showed me how powerful a dream can be."

"You did something amazing, Gilly!" said Lola. "You pushed us to be better, stronger, than we thought we could be."

"You all did it yourselves," she said. "You were the heroes, not me!"

The doors of the barn swung open. Gil and Kate Wells stood in the entry.

"You haven't moved since we left?" asked Gil. "Somebody may need to light a fire under you to get you moving, Punkin," he joked.

Gilly looked at Lola, who looked at Shadow, who looked at Gilly. They all laughed in cat tongue.

"Anything exciting happen while we were gone?" asked Kate.

"Not much," said Gilly, nonplussed.

"What happened to your cheek?" asked her mother with concern. "How did you get cut, Gilly?"

"Oh, I fell climbing the old apple tree in back. It's just a scratch from a branch." She rubbed her hand over the cut and took a deep breath to clear her head.

"Where are all the other cats?" asked her mother.

"Oh, they ran off. You know how fickle and unpredictable cats are, Mom," said Gilly with a lump in her throat. "Herding cats is like, well, herding cats!"

"I read that Zeke Meaner nearly won the Iditarod *again*," said Gil. "Aliy Zirkle beat him by mere seconds!"

Gilly snorted, and the cats both rolled their eyes. "He's lucky to be alive," she muttered.

"What?" said Gil.

"Nothing," said Gilly. And she hugged her parents, for she was very happy to see them. "What's for dinner?" she asked suddenly. "Lola and Shadow and I are famished! And Bolo too!"

Gil scratched the old dog behind his ears. "I bet you wish you could have run the race again, eh, old fella?"

"Nope," thought Bolo to himself. "Not this one."

Behind them, Gilly's sled lay tucked against the back wall of the barn. Its ash runners were scorched black, and the joints were wobbly, nearly pulled apart. Wrapped around the sled frame was a leather pouch with a few sparkles of glittering dust that glowed dimly in the waning light. A white feather of a snowy owl lay at the bottom of the sled.

As they were walking to the house, Gilly looked over her shoulder. In her mind's eye she saw Max sitting on the stone fence smiling like the Cheshire cat. He winked, leapt into the bushes, and was gone.

EPILOGUE

TEN YEARS LATER

Old Bolo died that next winter from old age. The years had taken their toll and he slipped away without any suffering. He was a natural leader, and Gil Wells said he never met a better dog in his life, nor ever would.

Max lives with his brother Willie in the White Mountains of Maine. They are the patriarchs of a colony of Maine coon cats and regularly get to the coast to enjoy the odd cod.

Ravi and Sasha live in the foothills of Bhutan. They spend their days watching trekkers slowly ascend the steps to the sacred Buddhist temples in the oxygen-thin air of the lofty Himalayas.

Che was last seen smuggling aboard a freighter bound for Nairobi. One report had him trudging across the Serengeti too late at night for his own good, with a pack of jackals howling in the distance.

Jami made it to Senegal. She settled with a family on the outskirts of Dakar near the coast where she can run in the sandy rolling plains. Sometimes at the end of the day, when the sun is setting in the west, she will look out over the Atlantic Ocean and remember her friends and their adventure in the wild snowfields of Alaska. Sometimes she will howl out over the sea at night and listen for a reply that does not come.

Simone lives beyond the Wrangell Mountains with her mate, Belloc, and three kits: Max, Sasha, and Ravi. Simone is a legend in the forest for her thrashing of Hugh the Wolverine and for teaming with the giant cats "the night the wolves turned tail."

  Gar made it back to South America and lived for a while in Colombia and then near the headwaters of the Amazon. After a few years, he traveled to Brazil and lived in Rio along the Copacabana. He was killed in a street fight near the Cristo Redentos, trying to defend an outnumbered stray cat against a pack of dogs.

  Lola and Shadow still live on the Wells property on the outskirts of Anchorage. They have the run of the barn, and although they are a bit slower on the pounce, there still aren't many mice or rats that dare cross their path. Since Gilly left for college, they often sit inside the house with Gil and Kate Wells beside the fireplace. It is a good life.

  Gilly is a student at Alaska Pacific University studying veterinary science with a minor in political science. Her senior thesis is titled "A comparative analysis of the cardiorespiratory VO2 max of felines and canines under competitive stress." She is on the Nordic ski team and has a colorful, happy circle of friends. They are all water rights activists and formed a club called "Stewards of the Earth." Sometimes, in the locker room, another woman will ask about the scars on her side and back. Gilly will smile and say "Australian crocodile." The opening quote in her journal is from the poet Ken Patchen, who wrote: "…there is nothing in the world but the Mystery."

TRIBUTE

This book is a tribute to all of the brave mushers and their faithful dogs who carried diphtheria serum across a forbidding wilderness in 1925, and to the racers who honor that epic journey in the modern Iditarod Dog Sled Race. In particular, we celebrate Libby Riddles, the first woman to win the Iditarod in 1985; the late Susan Butcher, who won the race four times; and Aliy Zirkle and the other female mushers who have challenged the conventions of their time. They belong among the intrepid adventurers and sportswomen—Amelia Earhart, Beryl Markham, Althea Gibson, Gertrude Ederle, Junko Tabei, Kay Cottee, Kathrine Switzer, Ann Bancroft, and others—who proved that aspiration, fortitude, and bravery have no gender. Their example should be empowering to all young people, girls and boys, who have dreams to pursue.

ACKNOWLEDGMENTS

The heroine of this tale is named after my dear niece Gillian. It was a genuine pleasure to work with the gifted illustrator, Elisabeth Alba, whose artistry captures the mystery of this adventure in a unique and lovely fashion. I am indebted to my friends Jon Waterman and Stephanie Joalland for their editorial expertise and wise literary advice. I am grateful to the staff of Hillcrest Media, especially editor Kate Ankofski, for guidance and counseling throughout the publishing process. My brother, Scott, a veterinarian in Missoula, Montana, was my guru on all things avian, feline, and canine.

I am eternally devoted to my late mother, Eugenia Ouren Ulvestad ("Lair of the Wolf") Bovard, and my father, the Honorable Gilbert K. ("Old Crow") Bovard, of Clear Lake, Iowa, for the blessings of a childhood filled with books, privilege, and love. I am indebted to my dear wife, Marnie, for her patience, creative input, and unwavering support. Marnie's beloved sable cat, Shade (the inspiration for Shadow), was a devoted companion for twenty-one years, and died during the writing of this story.

ABOUT THE ARTIST

Elisabeth Alba is an illustrator of fantasy, new age, children's, and middle-grade publications for such clients as Scholastic, Llewellyn Worldwide, and Simon & Schuster. She lives in Western Massachusetts with her husband, artist Scott Murphy. Elisabeth enjoys reading, traveling, running, and skiing, and hopes to take up cat sledding soon.

ABOUT THE AUTHOR

R. S. Bovard earned a bachelor's degree in literature from St. Olaf College, studied Shakespeare at Oxford, and later earned a medical degree at the University of Minnesota. While a medical student, he spent three months as a research assistant in an altitude-and-cold injury study on Mount McKinley (Denali), Alaska. Since then he has served as a missionary doctor in Papua New Guinea, as a ship's doctor for a Woods Hole SEA research schooner, an Everest expedition doctor, an Aspen ski clinic physician, a set doc on the films *Cliffhanger* and *The River Wild*, and a base physician at Palmer Station in Antarctica. He is a Masters swimmer and Nordic skier. He lives in Minneapolis, Minnesota, with his wife, Marnie, and two rascal cats, Lola and Bo.

CPSIA information can be obtained
at www.ICGtesting.com
Printed in the USA
FSHW010206040120